DARE TO KISS YOU

JULIA JARRETT

CONTENTS

Authors Note

This story was originally published as a holiday novella titled Lovestruck. It has been extensively revised and expanded into the story you are about to read. I hope you enjoy this version of Kat and Hunter's love story.

Please be aware, this book covers the sensitive subject of anxiety, and has a main character who suffers on page anxiety attacks. Everyone experiences mental illness differently, and what is described within these pages is based on my own experiences and interpretations. Please proceed with sensitivity and grace, for yourself and for anyone you may know struggling with their mental health.

Chapter One

Kat

You would think having four older brothers would mean someone else could rake the mountain of leaves that always fall in my front yard each autumn, but no.

No, and not because one brother lives in Montana, playing hockey in the NHL, another works insane shifts at the fire department, the third is a busy pediatrician at the hospital, and the last is an accountant who's working his butt off trying to obtain a partnership at his firm.

Rather, it's because my mom didn't raise me to be the kind of girl who is afraid to get her hands dirty. Nope, growing up I worked just as hard as the boys at any and all household chores. I can change a tire, do basic home maintenance, and yard work.

But I hate raking leaves.

Seriously, it's the most futile task ever. You rake them, more fall. Rinse and repeat. *Fucking leaves.*

Which is why every year, I find myself wishing I could somehow rope a brother or two into helping. Because while I love the gigantic maple tree that dominates my front yard, I don't love the cleanup it requires every fall.

"Need any help?"

A deep voice penetrates through my grumbling thoughts. The voice that I hear in my dirtiest dreams, *the dreams I really shouldn't be having about another man, seeing as I've got a boyfriend*. Granted, a boyfriend who lives halfway across the country and I don't get to see very often, but still. It's his voice I should be dreaming about, not the voice of the incredibly hot cop who moved in next door just over a year ago.

"Hey, Hunter," I say casually, turning to him. My greedy, guilty eyes take in his shoulders, covered in a snug fitting T-shirt. He's muscular, but in a sleek, athletic way, not a gym junkie way. I sweep my gaze over him quickly — his dark brown hair that is always messy, his eyes that constantly sparkle, and those full lips that never seem to stop smiling.

You know those people who seem to *always* be happy, no matter what? That's Hunter Callaghan. My cousin Leo works with him at the police department. One time, while having drinks with my brothers and me, he said Hunter reminds him of a golden retriever. I can see that, but not in a bad way. Hunter is just naturally happy, friendly, easygoing, and...cute. Very cute.

He's friendly with everyone but I've always felt like he's maybe just a little bit *more* friendly with me. It started right after he moved in, when he saw me petting our neighbour's big orange cat who had free rein of the neighborhood.

"Is that your cat?" he asked.

"No, he belongs to the Singhs." I gestured to a house down the street. "But he's super friendly."

"Cool." He sauntered over, sank down, and started petting the cat with me. Sure enough, Marmalade leaned into Hunter's

touch, purring nonstop. Lucky cat.

Hunter stood up and thrust his hands in his pockets before giv-ing me a grin. "Well, I better get ready for work. See ya around, Kitty Kat." He winked, then walked away.

At first, I wasn't sure if the nickname and the wink was really for me or for the cat. But from that day on, Hunter called me Kitty Kat. Maybe I shouldn't have liked it as much as I did, especially since I had recently started dating someone; the same someone I should be thinking about right now instead of my hunky neighbour. The nickname implies a closeness between us, a connection I know is probably all in my head. But that moment with our neighbour's cat was the start of the secret crush I've had on Hunter Callaghan.

And now the man in question is standing in my yard, looking far too yummy for his — or my — own good.

Boyfriend. I have a boyfriend.

"That tree sure does make a mess." He grins, pushing back the lock of hair that always flops down over his forehead. "But I've got a couple hours before I'm due at the station. Want me to help?"

My mind battles between eagerly wanting to say yes just to have the help, and desperately wanting to have a good reason to say no. Because the guilt that comes along with my attraction to Hunter is overwhelming sometimes.

"Sure, that would be great."

I regret the words as soon as I say them. But then Hunter smiles, and I smile back, and suddenly I forget what I was meant to be doing. Instead, I stand there like an idiot, smiling, until he comes back with his own rake and a pair of work gloves.

"Cool. I'll start over here and meet you in the middle."
Hunter moves to start raking, then pauses and stares at me. "You
okay, Kitty Kat?"

"Yup, fine! Great. Thanks." I pivot, only to step on my rake
and have it snap up and almost hit me in the face. Only it doesn't
because a gloved hand stops it just in time.

"Easy there. No black eyes, 'kay?"

Oh Lord, he's so close I can feel the warm air from his breath
as he talks, his words a lighthearted rumble.

I force out a light laugh and reluctantly step away from him,
taking the rake. "Thanks. Again."

His smile is out in full force. "No prob. Let's get raking. I'll
have you know, I'm a fast leaf raker. Dare you to keep up." He
winks, and I can't help but smile at his enthusiasm for something as dreary as raking leaves. But then his words sink in. I've
never — *never* — backed down from a dare. You don't grow up
with four brothers without being brave enough to always accept
a dare.

"You dare me?"

He nods. "Yep. Dare you to keep up with my epically awesome raking skills." He turns and starts raking at a manic pace,
forcing a bark of laughter out of me. I turn to my side of the
yard and start to match his movements. "What do I get when I
beat you?"

"A high five?" he calls out.

"A high five isn't much of a prize."

"Hey, I give really good high fives."

I laugh again, only to be consumed with a wave of guilt. The
last time Tyson came to visit, he made an offhand comment

about Hunter living next door and how friendly we seemed with each other. I reassured him we were neighbours and nothing more. But the truth is, I can't deny the fact that I'm attracted to him.

We get to work, and to my surprise time flies by. Barely an hour later and my yard is raked, the leaves bagged up and set by the curb to be picked up on the next trash collection day.

"Wow. Thank you, Hunter." I turn to him, full of gratitude. My arms ache from all the work, but it's a pleasant sort of tired. And it's enough to take the edge off my usual nerves.

"No prob, Kitty Kat. But I didn't notice who won the dare." He grins, leaning his rake against the tree, and taking off his gloves as he comes closer.

"Let's call it a tie?"

He lifts a hand and wiggles his fingers. "High five?"

I slap my hand against his, then let it fall to my side, suddenly unsure what to say or do now. Do I offer him a snack or a drink? Stay and make small talk?

But before I can overthink things, Hunter speaks. "I better go get ready for work."

I clutch my own work gloves with both hands, somewhat embarrassed that I was actually considering asking him to stay for a drink. Of course, he has to work. He even said that before we started.

Besides, what the hell am I doing, even considering asking him to stay? I. Have. A. Boyfriend. Not to mention I'm sure that to Hunter, this was nothing more than being neighbourly.

"Of course. Well, thanks again."

Because I'm looking anywhere *but* at him, I don't notice his arm lifting until I feel the lightest of touches in my hair. My head shoots up to see Hunter holding a leaf out in front of him.

"This one didn't want to go, I guess." He winks. "Bad leaf."

After he leaves, I go inside and get in the shower. Closing my eyes under the steady stream of water, my mind returns, unbidden, to Hunter lifting the leaf out of my hair. It's the first time over the year he's lived next door that we've come that close to each other. And I'm ashamed to admit my heart beat a little faster.

I shake my head and make myself think of Tyson instead.

Even though I haven't seen him in months, thanks to his temporary work assignment in another province, we decided to try long-distance. It's been hard, and the visits haven't been as frequent as I had hoped, mostly because of my school commitments. But he keeps saying he plans to move to Westport when he's done in Manitoba so we can be closer to each other.

So, I just put my head down, focus on finishing school, and hold onto the promise of that future. Which means *not* letting my conscious mind think about another guy.

My unconscious mind, however, I have no control over. Hence, the way I dream about Hunter — and then see him in real life.

I need to talk to Tyson. Maybe if I see him, hear his voice reminding me that we'll be together in the new year, just a few short months from now, I'll be able to put these pesky thoughts of Hunter out of my head.

When I'm dried off and wearing some comfy pajamas, even though it's early evening, I pour a glass of wine before sitting down on my couch and picking up my phone. I hit the button for a video call to Tyson and take a sip of wine.

The call connects, but I'm not looking at my boyfriend. I'm staring at...the ceiling, maybe? Then the sounds start filtering in.

An awkwardly familiar grunt, the unmistakable sound of skin meeting skin in a disturbing rhythmic pattern, and then...

"Fuck yes, Carlie, fuck!"

"Oh my God, Tyson!" I yell, spilling my wine as I bolt upright.

My hand is making the phone shake as I hear muffled curses and then, there he is, messed-up hair and a frantic look in his eyes.

"Kat? Babe? What the..."

"Who's Kat?" An unfamiliar and most definitely female voice asks in the background.

"I...I can't believe this," I start, brokenly. "You're having sex with someone else. You're cheating on me."

This isn't happening. *This can't be real.* But it is.

"Kat, it isn't what it looks like." Tyson climbs out of bed, which was a big mistake, seeing as his clumsy movements give me a full-frontal view of his condom-covered dick and the messed-up sheets in the background where I assume Carlie waits.

"At least you're using protection," I say bitingly. "I guess it's been so long since *we* had sex I hopefully don't need to worry about disease."

"Kat, no."

"Just stop." I hold up my hand, barely fighting back the tears. "We're done. I hope you and *Carlie* are very happy." I don't hide the sarcasm or the pain dripping from my voice as I hang up the call.

My phone instantly starts ringing again, and I hit ignore. It happens again; I ignore it again. Finally, after the third attempt of my cheating asshole of an ex trying to get through to me, I turn my phone off completely.

Chugging back the rest of my glass of wine, I pause a minute and take stock of how I'm feeling.

Hurt, yes. But more than that, embarrassed.

I never thought once that Tyson would cheat. Maybe that was naïve of me, given the distance between us and the time between our visits. Maybe it was inevitable that he'd wander, needing attention from someone else. But I foolishly didn't think it would ever happen to me.

After all, he's the one who pursued me. He's the one who desperately begged me to try long-distance when he had to move. He said he loved me, and I said it back. The first time I'd ever said it to someone outside of my family.

My heart is broken; my confidence is shattered.

If this is what love feels like, I don't want it.

CHAPTER TWO

I set the weights back on the rack, relishing the tremors in my biceps. There's not much that feels better to me than a great workout. *Wow, Callaghan, that's cheesy as fuck.* Yep, but also true. Ever since my years on the high school football team, and the hours spent in a dingy basement gym that smelled like Satan's dirty underwear working out with my teammates, I've loved the feeling of pushing my body to the extreme.

The gym is where I work out not just my body, but my mind. It clears the cobwebs, calms the anxiety beast, focuses my thoughts, and helps me tackle the day in a way better headspace. It's also one of the few places where I know I'm on a level playing field with everyone around me. It doesn't take brains to work out, just brawn. And I've got plenty of that.

But lately, the one thing a good gym session has *not* done is burn off any of the pent-up energy that's constantly inside of me.

Energy that has been slowly building for over a year now. Ever since I moved in next door to Kat Donnelly.

Yeah, I'm talking about *that kind* of energy.

It doesn't matter how fast I run or how heavy I lift; I can't escape my never-ending fantasies of that dark-haired beauty. Her green eyes hold me captive every time I see her, and her smile is imprinted on my mind so firmly, I see it when I close my eyes.

Then again, it's more than just her looks that make her attractive. There's something about her that puts me at ease in an instant whenever she's near. With just one smile, I somehow always feel better about everything in my life. Better about *myself*. She probably has no clue, hell, I don't even know how she does it, but Kat is magic to me. A miracle. But one I know I'll always only get to look at and never have.

The day I moved in, I was struck by her beauty and personality. I wanted to ask her out so fucking badly, but I was a chickenshit and didn't do it right away. It was several months before I managed to work up the courage to decide to ask her out. I wasted that time trying not to make a fool of myself when I'd see her at home, or worse, in front of other people at the café where she worked. Then, the day before I was going to make my move, some preppy guy in a Tesla pulled into her driveway. Watching them greet each other made it clear to me she was off the market.

That effectively put the nail in the coffin that hides my feelings for Kat Donnelly.

"Hey bro, you about done with the thirties?"

I snap out of thoughts of Kat at the sound of Sawyer Donnelly's voice.

He's got even more muscles than I do, and he's a hotshot firefighter. And *not* the kind of guy who would appreciate me fantasizing about his little sister.

"Uh, yeah, go ahead." I step away from the weight bench, grabbing my towel and water bottle as I make my way over to the treadmill. Sawyer would fucking kill me if he knew what I was thinking about, so a little distance between us just makes sense.

Another guy from the Dogwood Cove FD comes in and joins Sawyer, the two of them joking about something from their last shift. Seriously, those firefighters have it lucky. Two barbecues and two sleeps, that's the joke at the police station. Meanwhile, us cops are on constant patrol. It might be a small sleepy town on the coast of Vancouver Island, but we're also responsible for a stretch of highway that gets its fair share of action.

Ignoring them, I turn up the volume on my music and the speed on the treadmill until I'm in a full-on sprint. Finally, my head clears of everything, including thoughts of Sawyer's little sister.

"Callaghan, settle something for me, would you?" Sawyer's voice cuts through my music, and I press pause on the treadmill to turn and face him.

"What's up?"

"Diaz here claims he meets the most women when he hits the bars in Victoria. I'm trying to convince him to give Westport a try. Why drive so far when we've got plenty of beautiful ladies close by? What do you think? Where does a young virile cop such as yourself go to find some company?" He leans onto the railing of my treadmill and wags his eyebrows up and down. "I'm guessing you're not lacking in that area."

Sometimes Sawyer is so over-the-top ridiculous I don't know how to respond. And this is definitely one of those times. I suspect he's not quite the player he makes himself out to be, but that's none of my business. And his question is one I really don't want to answer.

Not when the woman I can't get out of my head...is his little sister.

"I don't know, man. It's been a while since I went out just for a hookup," I answer lamely, wiping the sweat from my brow with a towel.

"Time to change that, my man. You're coming to the Dogwood Cove Animal Shelter gala that's coming up, right? So why don't you join us this weekend and we'll find dates?" Sawyer's friend — Diaz, I guess is his name — says, walking up to us with a grin.

The mention of the animal shelter makes me think of Kat. She volunteers there; I bet she's going to the gala with her boyfriend.

Lucky him.

I tune back into the conversation just in time to hear Diaz say something that gets my back up instantly.

"Or maybe I could just ask Sawyer's hot sister."

"Shut the fuck up about my sister," Sawyer barks out, glaring at his friend. Diaz's hands go up in defense, and I have to control my own urge to smash his face in for talking about Kat. "Kat's off-limits. Got it? Just because she's single now doesn't mean any of you fuckers are good enough for her."

My brain stutters on that one word. Single? Kat's single?

I desperately want to ask Sawyer what happened because the last I heard she was still with Tesla guy. But there's no way to find out what happened without raising suspicion. And hearing him berate Diaz only reinforces my belief that I can't go there.

I don't have a chance in hell of being good enough for her.

Someone like her deserves everything. A bright future with a guy who's just as amazing as she is.

And that guy is definitely not someone like me, with my barely controlled anxiety and a learning disability that didn't get diagnosed until I was a teenager.

I drop down onto a mat and start stretching, trying to force the unwelcome self-criticizing thoughts out of my head. It's taken me years to even begin to stop feeling like a total failure in life, and to acknowledge the fact that having anxiety is not my fault. It's just the way my brain is wired, and it's just something I have to live with.

But even with all the medication I've tried, the therapy, and all the work I've done, I still find myself feeling completely unworthy, especially when measured up against someone like Kat Donnelly. She's mentioned that she's working on a fucking master's degree. That's a hell of a big deal if you ask me. That takes brains, and commitment, and drive.

"Hunter, you're a hockey fan, right? You gotta see this, bro. Fuckin' NHL trades are wild this year."

Sawyer drops down to the floor beside me and holds his phone in front of my face.

I've never been a fast reader, so panic starts to claw at my throat. The words blur. There's no way I can read them.

"Huh. Yeah, cool."

"Cool? Dude, did you even read it? It's total bullshit. Man, my brother's gonna be so pissed to hear about this."

Despite the wave of anxiety crushing me, I manage to remember that Kat and Sawyer's brother plays for an NHL team in the states.

"Right. Totally sucks, hope it doesn't affect him. Listen, I gotta go." Hopefully, my vague as fuck response matches whatever Sawyer wanted me to read. Because by now the panic is building to an unmanageable amount. I need to get out of here, and fast.

I stand up abruptly, gathering all my stuff and heading for the door without saying goodbye. Then I proceed to berate myself the entire way to my car. I absolutely hate that I freak out like I just did, even if I did manage to keep it mostly in my head. At least I think I did. I can't let myself consider how Sawyer or Diaz might be reacting to my fleeing the gym right now. That will only make my anxiety worse.

But seriously, having the beginnings of a panic attack, especially over something so goddamn stupid like reading an article on someone's phone just makes me hate myself even more. The pressure of not wanting Sawyer to know how slow I am with reading; it was suffocating in that moment. I'm not proud of how I basically ran out of there like a total pansy, but when it comes to fight or flight, I've always been flight.

My breathing rate gradually slows as I practice the mental grounding exercises my therapist Audrey has taught me over the years.

With the eventual return to a calmer state of mind comes an unwelcome reminder of my reality.

It doesn't matter if Kat is single now. Sawyer said it himself: there's no way a small-town cop who's a mental nutcase and almost flunked out of high school could ever deserve someone like her.

Chapter Three

Kat

"Kat, can you take this salad to table three, please?"

"You betcha." I plaster a smile on my face that probably does nothing to hide my exhaustion from staying up way too late studying last night. Picking up the white ceramic bowl piled with organic greens and vegetables, I make my way over to the table, weaving through a packed Camille's café. I set the food down in front of the customer who ordered it, stifling a yawn.

I definitely should not have picked up these extra shifts, not right before the winter exam period for my master's degree in nursing. And definitely not when I've had a hard time sleeping these last couple of months, ever since the fateful day I found out Tyson was cheating on me. Hearing my ex say someone else's name and hearing the telltale slap of skin on skin isn't something I've been able to forget. Talk about nightmare inducing.

"Hey, Kitty Kat!"

My hand fumbles the water glass I'm carrying back to the counter to be washed, and it drops to the floor, thankfully only breaking into a few large pieces.

"Shit," I mumble as I drop to the floor to start cleaning up the mess. I was really hoping not to see Hunter, today of all days, with my unwashed hair and bags under my eyes. Although, truth be told, I've been actively avoiding him as much as possible for almost two months.

Not so easy when you live next door to the person you're trying to avoid.

It's not fair to him, I know. He has no idea the mental turmoil I've put myself through since breaking up with Tyson. The guilt I felt at first that a teeny tiny part of me was relieved to end things with him, and the instant connection my mind drew between that guilt and my attraction to Hunter. Was it karma? Did the universe somehow know about my crush, and that's why I got to witness my ex cheating on me?

Logically, I know it's not true. Tyson was just a douche canoe. But still.

The last thing my heart needs is to get wrapped up in someone else. I need to focus on school, and that's it. After all, school can't hurt me the way a man could. I don't have to worry about whether school feels the same for me as I do for it.

"Whoa Kat, careful, don't cut yourself." Warm hands cover mine and I force myself to meet what I know are beautiful brown eyes, full of life and enthusiasm, as always.

As soon as I see his smile, the skin where we're connected starts to tingle. It all happens in a matter of seconds, but I snatch my hand away.

"I'm fine. Sorry. Just clumsy, you know?" I ramble, standing up quickly. But of course, Hunter's standing at the same time, and my head collides with his chin.

"Easy there, Kitty Kat." He laughs, but I'm too busy trying not to focus on how incredible it feels to have his hands steadying me. "You gotta stop trying to injure yourself around me or I'm gonna think it's my fault." His eyes are teasing and full of light.

I wish they were full of something else...something...dirty.

Oh my God. I mentally slap myself. This is exactly why I've been avoiding him.

"Sorry." I dump the broken glass in the garbage and reach for the dustpan and brush to finish the cleanup. "Are you staying in to eat today?"

"Nah, I gotta pick up for a few others today." Hunter smiles widely at me, a lock of his unruly hair falling over his forehead. Just like every other time I see it, I clench my fists to stop myself from pushing it back for him.

"Oh, okay. Did someone phone in the order?" I ask over my shoulder as I make quick work of finishing the cleanup. Hunter sinks onto one of the stools and watches me as I make my way back behind the long counter he normally sits at. His elbows land on the counter, hands propping his head up. God, he really is adorable. I forgot how easy it is to just talk to him and how good it feels to be around his upbeat energy.

"Leo did. So, are you ready for Christmas? I noticed the Singhs already have their lights up. It's still November, crazy early; am I right?" He winks, and I can't help but smile

"They're early every year. I wait till December. And as for being ready, nope, definitely not. But I will be once I get through exams," I say with a sigh as I start preparing the bag that will contain all the food he's taking back to the station.

Hunter winces. "How many do you have?"

"Just three. But one is in pharmacological interventions, and I am *not* looking forward to it."

"Dr. Donnelly is on her way," he teases, and I shake my head.

"Not doctor. My brother can be the doctor in the family; I'm happy with Kat Donnelly, nurse practitioner. And I'm a long way from that," I correct.

He lifts his shoulders and gives me a grin, but it doesn't quite reach his eyes, for some reason. "Same same but different? You're seriously smart, Kat, I'm sure you'll do great on your exams."

I hand him the bag full of sandwiches and soups for the cops on shift, hoping my blush isn't too noticeable. "Thanks, Hunter."

I wish I could say more, but I'm tongue-tied, just like every time he compliments me.

"See ya around, Kat." With a wave, Hunter walks out of the café, my eyes trailing after him, watching his perfect butt move in those uniform pants.

"Wipe your chin, you're drooling."

My head whips around to face my friend Lily, just as my hand comes to my face, in case she isn't joking. "Shush. Don't say that so loud."

Lily just rolls her eyes. "Seriously? The only person around here who doesn't know you're crushing on Hunter Callaghan, is Hunter Callaghan." She pauses, tilting her head to the side. "And your brothers, I guess."

"And they never will," I whisper fiercely, scrubbing the counter as I glare at her. "Because you are going to keep your mouth shut."

Lily scoffs. "As if your brothers would listen to me, anyway."

It's my turn to roll my eyes. Because she's got a point. We've been best friends since we were kids, which means my four older brothers have also known her since we were kids. And Lily is basically their second little sister.

"It doesn't matter, anyway. It's not like anything is ever going to happen with me and Hunter. I just don't need them knowing I like him that way. You know the boys would never let me hear the end of it; after what happened with Tyson, they seem more determined than ever to make me live my life as a spinster."

"I'm going to ignore the fact that you're letting your idiot brothers dictate your love life. Getting rid of Tyson was a blessing in disguise, and you know it. Even if it did hurt at the time. Besides, how can you say nothing's going to happen when you haven't given Hunter a chance? I see the way he looks at you sometimes, like a lost puppy who wants to follow you home." Lily giggles as she accepts the cup of tea I push across to her.

"What is it with everyone comparing Hunter to a dog," I mutter under my breath. "There's no point. Anything I feel for him is definitely one-sided."

"Um, first of all, you're wrong. Anyone looking at the guy can see the hearts in his eyes. And they've only become more obvious since you dumped the douche. But second of all, the point is, you could get laid. As your nearest and dearest friend, I happen to know it's been a while. After all, before video-gate, you hadn't even seen Tyson in how long, six months? Even if you don't want to date Hunter — which I don't think is the truth — you could just have some hot sex."

"Shh! Oh my God, Lily. Stop talking about my sex life, would you?" My eyes dart around, but thankfully, no one seems to be paying attention to my annoying best friend. "Besides, I don't want to *just* have sex with Hunter. Or with anyone, for that matter."

"Uh-huh, I don't believe you for a second." Lily folds her arms across her chest, staring at me. I'm filled with a mixture of dread and anticipation. "I dare you."

"What?" I freeze. She wouldn't.

Oh yes, she would. Because she was there throughout my childhood and knows this is the way to make me do something I'm afraid of. She was there when my first dare came from Jude. I was seven, and he dared me to jump from the high diving board at the local swimming pool. Ever since I felt the rush of pride and accomplishment after surfacing from the deep water, conquering my nerves so thoroughly, I've never turned down a dare.

"You can't resist a dare, Kat Donnelly. So, I dare you. I dare you to ask Hunter to the gala. That way, it's not a proper date, so there's less pressure." Lily looks at me triumphantly, making air quotes around the word *date*. "It's just two people going to the same event together." She spreads her hands out in front of her, as if she's magically solved all my problems. I open my mouth to respond, but she beats me to it. "Then maybe after the gala, he can give you some big O's. It's been a while, my friend. You know it, and I know it. And as your bestie, I'm telling you, it's time to get back on the horse. Or —" Lily waggles her eyebrows before leaning in and thankfully whispering "— the dick."

All I can do is shake my head. It isn't the first crazy thing Lily has said, and it won't be the last. "You're insane. And I hate you for using my inability to turn down a dare against me."

"Honestly, I don't know why I didn't think of this before. It's the only way to get your head out of the way and make you act. You broke up with Tyson over two months ago, and even before that, it's not like the relationship was going anywhere. I've watched you moon over Hunter Callaghan for way too long not to push you into this. And trust me, he moons, too."

"He moons, too? That's not even a proper sentence," I reply drily, still avoiding the acceptance of her dare, even though she knows — and I know — that I will. I'm also actively squashing the feelings that came up when she oh-so-kindly pointed out that my relationship with Tyson really wasn't the best. The end was coming for a long time, if I'm being honest.

Thank the freaking universe we're interrupted by the bells on the door ringing, signaling new customers. And as bold and crazy as Lily is, even she knows not to push this in front of others.

"I'm expecting your acceptance later tonight," she calls out merrily as she walks out of the café.

"Not happening," I reply before turning to take Hattie Henderson's order.

"What's not happening, dear?" the older woman asks, squinting at me from under yet another crazy hat. She always seems to have a new one; this time it's bright green with orange stripes.

"Nothing important, Hattie. Just Lily teasing me," I reply, hoping she accepts the vague answer.

I ring her up, and Hattie goes over to a table by the window, pulling out the paper I often see her in here with. She says she writes letters to her sister who lives on the mainland, which I think is adorable. But Mila says she thinks she's telling her sister all the Dogwood Cove gossip. Who knows, it's not like I'm ever a part of anything gossip worthy.

The rest of my shift goes by, and I stay busy enough that I don't have time to think about Lily's stupid dare.

But that evening, as I'm heating up some leftovers to eat before I make myself open my pharmacology textbook, I finally open the multiple text messages she's sent over the course of the day.

LILY: Dare.

LILY: I dare you.

LILY: you can't say no, you know you can't.

LILY: c'mon Kat, you'll thank me for this when you're having hot sex with Hunter.

LILY: Do it…

LILY: Also I know you're ignoring me. But I'm a parasite, I don't go away easily.

Chuckling, I finally type out a reply.

KAT: You're not a parasite. You're my well meaning but totally insane best friend.

LILY: Okay, thanks? But, you're gonna take my dare right?!

KAT: I'll think about it.

LILY: That's a yes! WOOHOO! That's my girl.

Even though she can't see me, I shake my head, knowing it's futile to try and fight her on this. I said I'd think about it, and I will.

Later. After I get through exams. It's times like this that I'm relieved I decided to waitress through school, instead of nursing. Sure, the ongoing experience in healthcare would be a good thing, but the lower stress and pressure of working at the café is what gives me the sanity and mental capacity to focus on my studies.

Walking through the doors of the Dogwood Cove Animal Shelter the next morning, I'm hit with the familiar sound of dogs barking. I knew when Mila Monroe and her husband Dr. Jackson Holt — the town veterinarian — said they were opening an animal shelter, I would be one of the first volunteers. Walking the shelter dogs and playing with the cats who are waiting for their forever homes a couple of times a week fills my cup with all the animal love I need. At least until I have the time for a pet of my own, of course.

When I get to the back room where volunteers and staff can store their things, Mila's there, tidying up the desk where we all sign in. She's my boss at Camille's café, and technically, my boss here, but Mila's never been anything but awesome.

"Hey Kat, how are you?"

"Good. Great." I yawn. "Okay, tired. I'm in study mode for the next couple of weeks until exams are over."

"Oh man, I don't envy you that. You're done before the fundraiser, right?"

The second annual Dogwood Cove Animal Shelter gala is coming up next month. It's a night when the town gets to put on their fancy clothes and have a party, along with a silent auction, all to try and raise more funds for the animal shelter. I missed it last year, thanks to my school schedule, but I'm looking forward to it this year. I nod. "Yeah, I'll be done a couple of days before, so if there's any last-minute stuff you need help with, just let me know."

She waves me off. "It's all good. You're busy enough with school, work, and here. I know, I'm one to talk, but from one workaholic to another, listen to me when I say, you deserve time to slow down and rest."

I laugh, but it's hollow-sounding. "Rest. What's that?"

Mila fixes me with a pointed look. "Exactly my point. Anyway, I'm outta here, Jackson and I are taking Milo and Annie for a hike." She pauses at the doorway. "Oh, make sure you visit the nursery. Jackson just finished checking over a mama cat and four kittens. They are the cutest little things."

That brings a smile to my face. There's nothing better than kittens. I desperately want one, but I just haven't brought myself to commit yet. A pet is a big deal, after all. "I will. Have a good hike, Mila."

"See ya, Kat. Oh, don't forget to let Rosie know if you're bringing a date to the fundraiser. She's in charge of seating. Right now, we've got you at a table with Lily and your brothers, but we still need to know who's bringing a date and who isn't. Just call her at Jackson's clinic."

Right. The gala fundraiser. The dare.

How could I forget.

CHAPTER FOUR

Hunter

"I can't believe you dragged me to the mall the first weekend of December."

I turn to Asher, my closest friend since middle school. "You didn't have to come, dude. I just told you I needed to go and grab a few things in Westport, and you decided to get in the car."

"You promised me dinner." He pouts like a child, instead of a grown-ass man.

"You sound like I'm taking you on a date, instead of this being you tagging along on my errands," I fire back.

"If it was a date, I'd be the best date you've had in a long time, buddy."

I grimace. Because he's right.

"When was the last time you were with a woman, anyway?" He noisily slurps the iced coffee he bought on the way here.

"Okay, Ash, I get it. I have no life. Thanks." I turn into the sporting goods store where I want to shop for some new runners. The shoes I've been wearing to the gym are getting pretty trashed, and it's time for a new pair.

We reach the wall of shoes, and there are so many people

around, it almost feels claustrophobic. Asher's right again, this is the worst time of year to be shopping. Thankfully, I find the brand and style I like, grab the sample, and then start looking for someone to help find my size. Glancing down at Asher, who's thumbing through something on his phone, I say, "You could help, you know. If we can find a salesperson, we can be done here."

"Then we get dinner?" Asher looks up at me skeptically. You'd never know the guy is some tech genius worth a ridiculous amount of money. Instead, he looks — and acts — like a teenage slacker with his oversized hoodie and ridiculous attitude.

"Yeah, yeah. Then we can go for dinner."

He pushes himself to stand and wanders off, hopefully in search of someone to help get my shoes. I look around again, but everyone wearing the distinctive red uniform of store staff is busy. Then my eyes land on a familiar head of shiny brown hair. I drop down onto the bench as soon as I realize Kat's here with Sawyer.

Of all her brothers, he's the one I worry about the most when it comes to someone finding out how I feel about Kat. He's the most vocal about his opinions on no one in town being good enough for her, and he's even louder about it ever since she broke up with the long-distance dude.

Or as I call him in my head, the dumbass who cheated on her.

That blew my mind when I heard Leo mention it at work one day. That idiot had the most amazing woman in the world, she was his, and he fucked around?

Damn fool.

Asher chooses that moment to come back, thankfully, with

a girl who, judging by the uniform and the harried look on her face, has been working hard all day.

"Here you go, dude. Get your shoes and let's get outta here."

I shoot him a glare, then turn to the girl. "Sorry about him. Can I please get these in a size twelve?"

She snaps her gum at me but takes the shoes without a word and disappears behind the wall of shoes, hopefully to find my size.

"Hey, isn't that Kat Donnelly?" Asher asks way too loudly.

I grab his arm and yank him down beside me, my face burning. "Shut the fuck up," I hiss. "Yes, that's her, and that's her brother. So, sit down."

"Is it the firefighter or the accountant? Because we could take the accountant, but the firefighter, no thanks, man. I'm out." Asher cranes his neck to the side. "That looks like the firefighter. He's built."

"I seriously need to stop telling you everything," I groan quietly. This wouldn't be the first time Asher's motormouth and lack of tact got us into trouble. Stealing a glance to the side, I inwardly sigh in relief when I don't see Kat and Sawyer anymore. "They're gone."

"So, you don't want to see her?" Asher asks and I stare at him for a second before he lifts his hands in surrender.

"I don't want to deal with her brother. That's all."

The salesperson returns with a box of shoes in hand. She gives them to me, and after opening them and double-checking sizes, I flash her a grateful smile.

"Let's go, Ash," I mutter to my friend. We make our way up to the checkout, and I'd be lying if I didn't admit my eyes are darting around looking for Kat. *Like a masochistic idiot.* I really don't want to face her brother, but I can't help it — I really *do* want to see her.

Hell, I always want to see her.

But there's no sign of either Donnelly as I pay, and Asher and I leave the store.

At the other end of the mall is a bar and grill that's part of a nationwide chain. The food is just okay, but they do at least carry local beers on tap, so that's where we head next.

But we don't get far before I hear a familiar voice. Just not the voice I actually wanted to hear.

"Callaghan!" Sawyer calls out, and I wince. Thank God he's behind me and can't see my face.

"Uh-oh," Asher mutters under his breath, the asshole.

I make my feet stop and turn around, plastering a grin on my face that doesn't falter even when I realize Kat isn't with him. "Hey, man. How's it goin'?"

"Great, just doing some Christmas shopping with my sister." Sawyer stumbles forward at that second, and the woman in question steps around him.

"Seriously, Sawyer? You couldn't wait two minutes for me to finish paying?"

I clear my throat. "Hey, Kitty Kat."

She whirls around, eyes wide. "Oh. Hunter. Hi." Fuck me, she sounds a touch breathless.

I wonder if she would sound like that in bed. Underneath me.

I don't even realize I'm drowning in the endless pools of her eyes until Asher shoves my shoulder, hard.

"We're heading for dinner at Robbie's. Want to join us?"

My head spins, exorcist style, to look at him. What the fuck is he doing inviting them? But even though I know hanging out with Kat and her brother would be an epic disaster, I still feel a pang of disappointment when Sawyer declines.

"Sorry, we gotta get back for family dinner tonight. Callaghan, see you at the gym sometime?"

I give some sort of reply that's obviously good enough because Sawyer and Kat turn and walk away, leaving Asher and I in the middle of the crowded mall.

"Seriously, dude? I haven't seen you this fucked over a woman since Becky the bitch."

I wince at that name. That's not a memory I need right now. "What the hell were you thinking, inviting them to the bar?"

"I was thinking this is the girl my buddy's interested in, and I could play wingman and hang with the brother while you get your groove on."

I stare at him. "You're fucking insane."

Asher just throws his arm over my shoulders and pulls me toward the bar. "I prefer engaging and enigmatic. Now, let's go. I'm hungry."

A short while later, we're sitting in a booth, a hockey game is playing on the television screens all around us, and two ice cold glasses of beer and a plate of nachos are on the table between us.

"You know I love you like a brother, right?" Asher starts, and when I move my gaze from the hockey game to him, I notice a strangely serious expression on his face.

I put my phone down. "Yeah. I know."

"So don't be mad at me when I say this. Why the fuck are you holding back from going after Kat? You said she's single now, so why not ask her out? And don't give me that shit about the first responder's code or whatever the fuck that was."

"You don't date a guy's ex, sister, or daughter," I say, automatically stating the words one of my colleagues told me on my first day. "Rules for working in a small town."

"Okay, but rules for *living* in a small town should trump that. Because wouldn't that basically make every woman off-limits?"

I consider that for a split second. "Maybe? I don't know. But it's not just that. She's way too good for me, man."

Asher scoffs. "Don't you fucking dare start with that again. You're a good guy, Hunter. At the risk of getting sappy and shit, you're a catch."

I duck my head and pick at the paper coaster my beer sits on. It's damp from condensation and shreds easily. Asher has known me since childhood. He knows all about my learning disability and my anxiety. He was there when the only serious girlfriend I've ever had shattered not only my heart, but also my confidence.

When I told him I was moving to Vancouver Island for work, it was only a few months before he sold his apartment in Vancouver and moved over as well. We're closer than brothers, and I know he's always got my back.

But the one thing he doesn't get is how deeply damaged I am. How fucked up my head can be sometimes, and how impossible it is to get out of the mental holes I dig myself into.

"Can you just drop it for now," I ask quietly.

He doesn't reply at first, and I chance a look up to see my best friend studying me intently. "Fine. But hear me out first. You can't keep holding yourself back. I don't know how to get you to see yourself the way everyone else does, but I sure as shit hope you learn how to soon. Because Hunter Callaghan is a good guy. And Hunter Callaghan deserves to be happy. And Hunter Callaghan needs to get laid. And Hunter Callaghan —"

I hold my hands up in surrender, fighting back a laugh. "Okay, okay, okay, I get it. Enough with the Ric Flair routine."

He stops and picks up his beer, tilting it toward me in acknowledgment. "As long as you repeat one thing for me."

"What?" I ask with some trepidation.

"Just say this: 'I'm worth it.'"

"I'm not L'Oréal," I deadpan. "How 'bout I buy the next round instead."

Asher rolls his eyes skyward. "You're impossible. But fine. Buy my beer."

Chapter Five

Kat

My mom is who I go to anytime I'm happy, sad, confused, overwhelmed, or all of the above at the same time. When I was working as a nurse in a busy trauma hospital on the mainland, feeling burned out and homesick, she's the one who reminded me of my childhood dream to be a nurse practitioner, with a focus on women's health, in our hometown.

Even though my oldest brother Max is the doctor in our family, it was Mom who helped me fill out my application to the University of Victoria's master of nursing program. She's the one I celebrated with when I got in, and she's the one who has provided me with all the late-night study snacks and a shoulder to cry on during my pre-exam freak outs.

But I can't bring myself to talk to her about my feelings for Hunter.

Yep, there I said it, *feelings*. I have feelings. As awful as it sounds, I think I have for some time now, but I never allowed myself to acknowledge them because I was committed to Tyson.

A lot of good that did me.

"Hi, honey." Mom's cheerful voice floats to me from the

kitchen as soon as I close the front door of my childhood home. "I'm just pulling the last batch of cookies out."

Once I've hung up my coat, I follow the smell of cinnamon and spice. Nobody makes gingerbread cookies like Claire Donnelly, and today is our annual cookie decorating marathon, while holiday movies or rom-coms, depending on our mood, play in the background.

"Hey, Mom." I lean in to give her a kiss before heading to the sink to wash my hands.

"I thought we'd start with gingerbread, then move on to the sugar cookies for your dad. Oh, and I found this new recipe we've got to try for meringue wreaths. They're just adorable."

"Sounds good to me. Want me to start the movie? What are we watching first?"

Mom dusts off her hands and bustles over to me, wrapping her arms around my shoulders for a quick hug. "Doesn't matter to me, sweetie. Oh, I meant to call you. Did you see the latest *Buzz Watch* article?"

I shake my head. "No, Mom, you're the only one obsessed with that tabloid," I tease. She shushes me with a gentle swat to my shoulder. "Well, listen to this. Charisma Cross, the romance author Paige wants to bring to her bookstore, was interviewed about her views on the double standards between men and women when it comes to embracing their sensual side."

Mom pulls up the article on her phone and hands it to me. My eyes skim the text, and I must admit, the woman has guts. She's not holding back.

I bet she'd be brave enough to ask the guy she likes to be her date for an event without needing to be dared to do so...

"This is great and all," I say, handing the phone back to my mom and avoiding her eyes. She knows me far too well. "But let's face it. Loads of people have said something like this before. It's not like this is magically going to end misogynism."

"Hey, we can hope for a Christmas miracle, can't we?" Mom replies drily and we both laugh. "But seriously, I think she's got a good message. You know, in my day, there were next to no places for women to safely explore their sexuality. I think it's great you can find these strip shows, and sex shops, and —"

"Oh my God, Mom, stop!" I cry out, covering my ears with my hands in mock panic. "I know we're close, but we are not strip show and sex shop close."

"Relax, Kat." Mom laughs, shaking her head at me. "I don't need the details of your intimate relations anymore than you need the details of mine. Past or present." Her wink makes me cringe ever so slightly.

I might have a deep respect and admiration for my parents' marriage, and want nothing more than to have something similar for myself someday, but thinking about their sex life? Nope. Not going there.

"The Walkie Talkies were discussing the animal shelter food drive, by the way. Did you know the police department is collecting donations? I nagged your brother to make sure the fire department does the same."

I fight back a snicker the same way I always do when Mom mentions her walking group. Their name is just too amusing, and she seems oblivious to it. "That's fantastic, we can definitely use it."

"I'm trying to convince your father we need a dog, but so far, he's not on board. Says the house is busy enough with all of you kids coming in and out."

"He's not wrong." It's true, my parents have always had an open door for any of us. Whether it's stopping by for dinner, grabbing some of Mom's baking, or just coming to visit, it seems one of us is always around.

"Anyway, back to the movie choices," I say, trying to refocus the conversation. "Are we jumping straight in with the corny Christmas movies, or starting with something different?"

"It's not Christmas cookie day if we don't watch at least one cheesy movie," Mom reasons.

"Deal."

With the movie on, we finally get to work decorating the dozens of gingerbread cookies Mom and I use as gifts for people in the town each year. It's a labour of love, that's for sure, but it's also a major stress reliever for me. Which right now, leading up to exam week, I need.

Several hours and too many cookies to count later, we're done. And with a steaming mug of mulled wine in hand, we each sink down on the couch in my parents' living room.

"Phew. I swear, every year I tell myself this is it, no more cookies. And every year, we find ourselves here again, covered in flour and sprinkles."

"Come on, Mom. You love it." I nudge her with my foot.

"I do, but it's not the cookies. It's spending time with my girl." Her hand pats my leg. "It's only a matter of time before you find someone, fall madly in love, and start making your own traditions. Then, days like this will be just a fond memory."

I snort lightly. "There are so many things wrong with what

you just said. First of all, I don't care what's going on in my life, I will *always* want to have cookie day with you. And second of all, just who am I going to fall madly in love with? Look at how well that turned out with Tyson. Besides, there's not exactly a lot of prospects in Dogwood Cove, not when almost every guy my age has already been scared off by the boys."

"Tyson was not worth the dirt he stands on," Mom deadpans. "And don't be so hard on your brothers, they just want you to be happy."

"Then maybe they should back off a little," I grumble, taking a sip of my mulled wine.

"Is there someone in particular you're hoping they'll back off on?" she asks, giving me an innocent-looking smile.

"No, nope. Of course not. No one," I answer quickly, avoiding her curious gaze. Dang it, her mom radar is pinging, I just know it.

"It would be okay if there was, my sweet girl. It's been a few months since...*the incident*." I hide my smile at how she lowers her voice to say that. "No one would think any less of you if you started putting yourself out there."

"I know," I say quietly, knowing she's right. Truthfully, Tyson only came to town twice, so it's not as if people really knew him at all. Heck, I bet a lot of people never realized I was in a relationship to begin with.

"Are you and Lily going to the animal shelter gala together, then?"

"Well, actually, there is someone I want to ask, but I'm scared the boys will just scare him off," I blurt out, wincing at my confession. Okay, my partial confession. Worrying about my brothers is only half of my reluctance, the other half is this deep-seated fear that Hunter might say no.

"Oh honey, your brothers mean well. But if you want them to back off, just tell them that."

"I have," I grumble. "Every single time they interfered with a guy I was dating or interested in, I told them to stay out of it, and they never do."

"Well, any man worthy of you would be plenty strong enough to stand up to the boys."

I take another sip of my warm drink, and cautiously, slowly, allow myself to imagine the reality in which I actually ask Hunter to go as my date to the gala. More importantly, I imagine the possibility of him saying yes.

It's scary. Really scary. To think about putting myself out there again brings up unfamiliar and uncomfortable questions of self-doubt. If I wasn't enough for my ex, what's to say I'm enough for anyone? What if Lily's wrong and Hunter isn't into me? What if my crush for him is completely one-sided and he sees me as nothing more than a neighbour and the woman who serves him soup and sandwiches?

Still, the thing is, Lily hasn't stopped bugging me about her stupid dare for days. I've never backed down from a dare, not since we were kids. She knows it's the only way, when I'm nervous, to get me to just push through the fear and do something. And maybe this time, it's exactly the nudge I need.

"I know you've been focused on school, and work, and your future. But don't forget, you're entitled to have a little fun in life. Okay, sweetie? And if that fun happens to come wrapped up in a big, burly man, all the better."

I rest my head on my mom's shoulder, soaking in the comfort she's offering.

"Thanks, Mom."

"So, you'll think about asking this mystery guy?"

There's no more thinking to be done. Because Lily's right, I've never backed down from a dare. I have to push through my fear that Hunter doesn't want me the way I want him, and just do it.

I'm going to ask Hunter to the gala.

Of course, as luck would have it, it's several days later before I finally see Hunter at the café. We keep missing each other at our houses, his driveway being empty when I'm home, and I can only assume that I've been at my exams or work when he's been home.

There's nothing unusual about that; we've gone days or even a week between seeing each other in the past, and it's never bothered me.

Okay, fine, maybe that's because before now, I was in a relationship. And even if my ex didn't take that seriously, I did. I might have been attracted to Hunter, but I never in a million years considered acting on that attraction. So, if we were two ships passing in the night, that didn't matter because we were just neighbours.

Only now, I'm single. He's single. And I want to ask him to the gala. Now, not seeing him is driving me a little crazy because every day that goes by when I don't get the opportunity to ask him, I end up feeling more and more on edge. And the more on edge I get, the more annoyed I get with myself for letting my ex damage my self-esteem so much.

I have to continually remind myself there's no real reason not to ask Hunter to go with me to the fundraiser. Except my fear that maybe I've imagined his flirting, or maybe Lily's wrong and he doesn't look at me with hearts in his eyes. Maybe I'm making something out of nothing, and he has zero interest in me whatsoever.

But I've gone after everything else I want in life, without hesitation. So why not this? The worst that could happen is he says no. And as long as I keep reminding myself there's no emotions involved — yet — I'll be okay. My heart will stay intact. Sure, that might make it awkward living next to him, but I'm a big girl. I can handle it.

Of course, when I finally see Hunter walk through the door of Camille's, looking as delicious in his uniform as he always does, the nervous feeling in my stomach turns from cute little butterflies to a full-on tornado. So much for keeping emotions out of it.

I make my way over to him, grateful the café isn't too busy right now and even more grateful he's here alone and not with my cousin. Less witnesses if this all goes horribly wrong and he says no.

"Hey, Kitty Kat," he says, giving me that adorable smile, the one that makes the dimple in his cheek pop. That errant lock of hair has flopped over his forehead again, and I focus my eyes there.

"Hi, Hunter." Oh God, why is my voice so high-pitched? I

clear my throat and try again. "Hi. Um, are you staying for lunch today?"

He nods, still smiling his perfect smile. If anything, it grows wider. "Yep. Why? Are you on a break? Am I finally going to get the pleasure of your company for more than the thirty seconds it takes you to drop off my sandwich?"

He's teasing, I'm sure of this, but man, oh man, do I want him to be serious about wanting my company.

"No, no break, sorry," I answer haltingly, and I swear for just a second his smile falters. But only for a flash and then he's back to his usual happy self. Probably hiding his laughter at my fumbles. Why am I tongue-tied around him?

I take a deep breath, knowing if I don't ask him now, I never will.

"Hunter, do you want to go to the animal shelter fundraiser gala with me?"

There's a stunned look on his face for a moment before he starts nodding vigorously. So vigorously, his hair starts flopping all over the place, and I can't contain my giggle of pure relief.

Maybe, just maybe, Hunter Callaghan *is* interested in more than friendship with me. Maybe I'm not alone in this crush after all.

CHAPTER SIX

Hunter

I can't stop staring at a string of numbers.

Just ten fucking numbers.

But those ten numbers? They're Kat Donnelly's phone number.

And I have it at last.

Granted, as her neighbor, I had a good enough reason to get her number a long time ago. I just never had the guts to ask for it and she never offered.

Until now.

After she asked me to go to the gala, the damn voice in my head told me she was joking. It had to be a joke.

Except, I know Kat would never be cruel and play with someone's feelings like that. Not with how kind she is to everyone around her. Hell, her smile might be magic for me, but I also know she helps Hattie Henderson when she forgets her reading glasses and can't see the specials on the board. I've caught her drawing pictures on the back side of receipts and giving them to kids who come to the café. Kat cares about people. She doesn't judge, or get impatient, or make fun of anyone.

Which means her inviting me to the fundraiser was no joke.

Add in the fact that she's now single, and I can't stop wondering if the invitation was just for two friendly neighbours to go to a party together, or more. Which is what has been fueling my chaotic thoughts, causing me to feel the entire spectrum of emotions. Everything from the initial shock when she first asked, to utter panic over the fact that now I need to buy a suit, to questioning if Kat might actually be interested in me, to *excitement* that Kat might be interested in me...

That last emotion? That's the one that kept me up last night, eventually needing my hand and a cold shower to be able to fall asleep.

"Planning on joining us, Callaghan?" Leo Talbot, my boss — and Kat's cousin — says drily from his place at the front of the conference room inside the Dogwood Cove police station.

"Yes, sorry. I'm here." I flip my phone over and give him an apologetic grin. Thankfully, Leo's a cool guy and doesn't give me shit for not paying attention during our daily staff meeting. But he does stick me with highway patrol for the day, which normally would have me groaning inwardly.

"Okay, and before we get started, let me remind you all that interviews for the two new detective positions are starting soon. If you want to be considered, I need applications submitted by the end of the week." Leo fixes me with another stare, this one making me squirm in my seat.

He's mentioned in passing that I should submit an application. But I haven't. And I don't intend to. After all, there's not a chance in hell I'd be the best candidate for the promotion. Why bother setting myself up for disappointment? I have enough of that swirling in my head in the form of self-criticism. The last thing I need is for my superiors to tell me I'm not good enough. I already know that.

After the meeting ends, I avoid Leo and take one of the SUVs out of the lot and make my way to the highway as snow falls around me, blanketing the ground. We don't get heavy snowfall very often on Vancouver Island, so every time we do, there's always a handful of drivers who are not equipped for it and cause all kinds of issues on the roads.

Don't get me wrong, I love the snow, but only when I don't have to work in it. Give me a mountain to ski down and a hot tub waiting at the bottom any day. But this? Rescuing stranded, unprepared idiots over and over again? No, thanks.

The next several hours fly by as I keep having to pull over to help push cars that have spun out on the road, call tow trucks for ones that just can't handle the winter weather, and even attend the scene of one crash. Thankfully, no one has been hurt so far, but I'm cold and cranky. Why don't people learn from their mistakes and get winter tires before it's too late?

I've just sent the third tow truck on its way, this time with a little convertible hooked up to it and a shaken driver who promised me they were headed straight to the tire shop tomorrow. I waved the snowplow along gratefully, when out of the corner of my eye, I catch the blinking of someone's hazard lights behind me about fifty meters. I grab my first aid kit, just in case, and radio in my location and that I'm leaving my patrol car before heading out on foot down the highway. It's starting to get dark out, and while the snow has slowed down, it's still pretty blustery out here. Thank fuck, my shift is almost over. I can probably head back to the station after I deal with this car and its occupants.

But when I finally make it through the snow drifts on the passenger side and peer in the window, my heart leaps into my throat at the sight of a familiar head of glossy dark hair bent over. I pound on the glass, making the driver look up in surprise.

She presses the unlock switch for the doors and I quickly get in, my eyes searching Kat's body frantically for any signs of injury. "Are you okay?"

She huffs out a sigh. "Hi, Hunter. I'm fine, but my stupid heater isn't working."

I turn some dials, and sure enough, there's no heat coming out of the vents.

"Shit. That's not good, Kitty Kat. Why didn't you keep driving home?"

Her head thumps back against the headrest. "I pulled over to see if I could get it working again, instead of messing around while I was driving, and then had the brilliant idea to turn the car off and on again. You know, like you do with electronics. Restart and all that shit. But now the car won't start."

The mixture of sarcasm and frustration in her words makes my mouth quirk up in a small grin, but the truth is, I'm still fighting back waves of anxiety. If I hadn't been close by, how long would Kat have been stuck here?

"Before you start giving me hell, I was just having a moment of self-pity before calling my brother when you walked up. And I have emergency blankets in the back, so I'd be warm until he got here."

I huff out a laugh at her sass as the waves of panic slowly

subside. "Busted. I was totally gearing up to read you the riot act about winter preparedness. Why don't I give you a ride home? I'm off shift now and it would be a lot faster than waiting for your brother."

She blows air out between her lips and rolls her head toward me. "Yeah, that would be great, thanks." Her grateful smile warms the air between us and my hand sneaks out to tuck a strand of hair behind her ear. When she laughs at my action, I snatch my hand back.

"Sorry," I mumble, feeling like an idiot.

"Don't apologize. I'm only laughing because you have no idea how many times I've had to stop myself from doing that to *you.*"

My embarrassment turns into confusion until she reaches out, removes the toque from my head, and twirls the lock of hair that is always in my eyes around her finger. Only then do I let out a chuckle of my own. She wasn't making fun of me. Fucking anxiety.

"Thanks." I pull my hat back on. "But what do you mean you've had to stop yourself?"

Kat tugs her lower lip between her teeth and her eyes drop down to her hands.

"Because I...I didn't think we were like that. I mean, we're friendly, sure, but you're friendly with everyone. I didn't want you to feel like I was being too forward."

"You didn't want to be too forward and touch my hair, but you have no problem asking me to be your date to a fancy dinner?" I pull on my humour to dispel the last few tendrils of worry and embarrassment swirling inside me.

Her face turns pink, but she giggles. "Yeah, I never claimed to be smart."

The radio strapped to my shoulder chooses that moment to come to life, dispatch informing me I'm officially off shift and should return to the station. My replacement is on their way. After I give my confirmation and inform them I'm on my way back to station, I turn to Kat.

"Ready to go? Or would you like to hang out in this icebox for a while longer?"

Her laughter tells me I've made the right call by infusing the situation with jokes. I'll take having Kat as a friend, even if I wish things were different — *I was different* — and we could be more.

But I know from past experiences that women like Kat, women who have their future planned out with goals and dreams, don't want guys who will never be more than a regular old police officer with zero chance of moving up in rank.

Because you'd have to apply for promotions in order to get them.

Together, we collect her belongings and make our way back to my patrol car. Moments later, we're back on the highway, slowly making our way toward town.

Once we're in the warmth of my car, Kat removes her heavy winter coat, twisting her upper body to put it behind us. The action brings her close to me, and I get a whiff of her shampoo, some sort of fresh tropical smell. Her shoulder brushes mine as she turns to face forward and I shift in my seat, gripping the steering wheel tightly. We've never been in such close quarters. This is going to be torture.

"Thanks for this, Hunter," she says quietly, and I chance a quick look at her. She's watching me.

"Of course. It's my job to save helpless maidens, you know," I reply, continuing with my jokes. Humour has been my defense mechanism for so long, it's just natural when I feel out of my element.

And being this close to Kat? I'm *definitely* out of my element.

"I'm going to ignore the helpless maiden part of that, and just say I know it's your job, but I'm still really glad it was you who came to my rescue."

My dumbass heart flip-flops around in my chest. That stupid organ doesn't know any better; doesn't know Kat Donnelly is not for us.

"I'm glad it was me, too." The words slip out, quieter and more serious than anything else I've said so far.

All too soon, we're pulling into Dogwood Cove and cruising down the street toward our two houses.

"Want me to shovel your driveway when I get back from the station?" I ask, half hoping she'll say yes, half hoping she won't because I *hate* shoveling snow.

"No, that's okay. Beckett said he's coming to do it after he finishes Mom and Dad's house."

"Okay."

Kat hesitates, her coat and bag in her arms.

Ask her out, you dumbass. But I don't.

Instead, I just sit there as she climbs out of my patrol car and leans back down through the open door. "Thanks again, Hunter."

"No problem."

I watch her walk up to her front door, open it, and close it behind her without ever looking back at my car. Only then do I drop my head to the steering wheel with a loud thunk.

"You are a fucking coward, Hunter Callaghan."

And I have been ever since I was seventeen.

The last time I let myself get involved romantically with anyone.

The first time I realized my struggles might not have been my *fault*, but they would forever make me less than anyone else who didn't have them.

Chapter Seven

"Is this stupid? Maybe this is stupid. How ridiculously corny is it to drop off Christmas cookies as a thank you?"

"Be honest, Kat, those cookies are more than just a thank you," Lily waggles her eyebrows at me through the phone screen.

"Remind me again why I called you?" I ask drily.

"Because you were getting cold feet, and as your best friend, I'm the perfect person to tell you to woman up and give the man your cookies. And I'm not just talking about the ones you're baking."

"Good grief, Lil." I can feel the heat flushing my cheeks. I'm no prude, but Lily takes her brazenness to a whole other level.

"You love me, and you know it. Now, tell me again about how he was your knight in shining police uniform. I swear, you two are living my secret crush fantasy."

"*I'm* living your fantasy? Having feelings for someone and obsessing over the fact they might not be returned? Girl, you've got issues." I place the last ball of cookie dough on the sheet and put it in the oven. "Besides, since when do you keep secrets from me? Who's keeping you up at night and why have you not told me?"

Lily's eyes shift away from her screen. That's odd. I was only joking, but it seems like I've landed on something.

"Lil?"

"I was just teasing you. There's nobody. As if I could keep a secret from you." Her laughter sounds way too forced, but I don't push the issue. Not when I'm starting to panic that in twenty short minutes, the cookies will be done. Then I'll have nothing left to delay this harebrained idea I had to take Hunter some home baked goodies as a thank you for helping me the other day.

"We'll revisit that later. Right now, what the heck do I wear?"

"A trench coat with nothing underneath?"

"Seriously, Lily," I groan. "Enough already. I'm not going over there for sex. I'm going to say thank you."

"And I'm just saying the perfect thank you *is* sex. Besides, it's Christmas. Consider it your Christmas present to him as well."

"I'm going to hang up now."

Lily's hand goes up in surrender. "Fine, fine, I'll stop. As long as you promise to wear something just a *little* bit sexy. Can't hurt, can it?"

"Sometimes I wonder how we became best friends," I say teasingly as I carry my phone down the hall to my bedroom.

"Easy. You tame my crazy side and I encourage your sassy side."

A little while later, I'm chewing on my thumbnail and staring at a tin of cookies, trying to work up the courage to text Hunter.

You'd think asking him to the gala would have taken the edge off my nerves, but it hasn't. If anything, him saying yes only made things worse. Because now I know there's a chance he's interested in me. A chance. Not confirmation, just a chance.

So, what if he thinks we're just going as friends, when I want it to be more? With a sharp exhale, I press send on my message.

KAT: Hey, Hunter, it's Kat. If you're home, I wanted to drop off some Christmas cookies I baked as a thank you for helping me when my car broke down.

I've deleted and retyped it at least three times, trying to figure out how to not sound like a weirdo who happens to know he's home because I can see his car in the driveway. Not that I've been checking obsessively for the last two hours while the cookies baked or anything.

It's only been the last hour.

Yeah. Stalker mode engaged.

Almost immediately, I see those three dancing dots that mean he's replying.

HUNTER: Hey Kitty Kat! Yeah I'm home. Come on over.

Well, okay then. Here goes nothing. I pull on my coat and boots, then pick up the box of cookies and trudge through the snow down my driveway and over to his, then along the shoveled path to his house.

When Hunter opens the front door and I see his huge grin, that dimple popping and his eyes twinkling, my nerves some-how disappear.

"Hi," I say softly, holding out the box of cookies. "Thank you again for helping me the other day." He goes to open his mouth and I hold my other hand up. "I know you're going to say it was your job, but I'm still saying thank you. So just take the cookies, okay?"

"Only if you come in and eat some with me."

My heart jumps. "Oh — okay."

He stands back and I walk past him into his house. Despite being neighbors for a while now, I've never been inside.

As I pass, our bodies brush against each other and I get a hint of that unmistakable Hunter scent. Fresh and woodsy, all at the same time, and enough to stir up all kinds of pheromones in my body.

"Here, ah, make yourself comfortable. I'll just..." Hunter drops his gaze as he bustles past me, straightening pillows and picking up a coffee cup that was on the table. His house is surprisingly clean, so I'm not exactly sure why he thinks he needs to tidy up.

"Can I get you a drink? I've got water, coffee, beer, or milk."

"Milk?" I ask, surprised by that offer.

Hunter just grins. "What else would I put out for Santa on Christmas Eve?"

A couple of minutes later, he walks over and sets down two glasses of cold milk on the coffee table before sitting down on the couch beside me.

"I decided Christmas cookies need milk. Hope that's alright with you."

I nod, smiling. Hunter opens the box of cookies I brought, and his eyes widen. "Wow, Kat. These look incredible!"

He pulls out an iced Santa hat sugar cookie and looks at me

with wonder. "You did this?"

"Yup. My Mom and I do a ton of iced cookies every year. The chocolate crinkles I made fresh this morning."

"Chocolate crinkles are my *favourite*," he says reverently, putting the Santa hat away and digging for the chocolate cookie. His eyes fall shut as he takes a bite and moans. "Ohhh. So good." Crumbs fall from his mouth, and he looks at me sheepishly as he wipes them away. "Sorry, I haven't had these in years."

"It's okay." I laugh. "I'm glad you're enjoying them." I pick up a raspberry jam thumbprint cookie and nibble at it. Hunter demolishes his first cookie and grabs a second, making quick work of that one as well.

"I was really happy you asked me to go with you to the animal shelter fundraiser."

I look over at Hunter in surprise. He sounds hesitant, and for the life of me, I cannot figure out why.

"Oh! Well, thank you for saying yes," I reply, feeling my own version of awkward. This feels like we're teenagers, with zero social skills, dancing around our feelings for each other. The image of me in braces and glasses, frizzy hair and zero fashion sense makes me laugh under my breath. Because the reality is, Hunter probably wouldn't have given me the time of day, much less agreed to go to a party with me. Thank goodness, grown-up me has a few things figured out, like hair products.

"What's funny? Do I have crumbs on my face?" Hunter wipes at his chin, looking embarrassed, and I put my hand on his wrist to stop him. The instant we make contact, we both freeze, staring at each other.

"No, no, you're fine," I reassure him. My lip gets tugged

between my teeth and I feel a blush creep over my cheeks. "I was just thinking about what it might have been like if we knew each other when we were younger."

His eyebrows lift. "And it was that funny?"

"Well, I don't know about you, but I was a hardcore nerd. Big glasses, fuzzy hair, braces — it was not a good look. You probably wouldn't have even noticed me."

"I would have noticed you."

The words come out so quietly I almost miss them, but I don't miss the intense heat in his gaze.

I can no longer deny that things are shifting between us. He's still the hunky neighbour I've crushed on, but now I'm letting myself see beyond that. Beyond the sexy man I've been denying my attraction to. I'm starting to get glimpses of the man beneath the good looks and upbeat personality. His vulnerabilities that I get the feeling he doesn't show very often, his soft side, his caring side. He's more than just the happy-go-lucky Hunter.

I want to know more.

I want to know all of him.

The problem is, does he want all of me?

Chapter Eight

Hunter

When I was hired by the Dogwood Cove Police Department, I chose to disclose my learning disability to the chief. Mostly because I wanted the ability to provide my reports dictated and typed instead of handwritten. Thankfully, they were more than happy to accommodate my request, and so far, I have yet to receive any criticism or judgment from my coworkers.

But that means it takes me longer to finish everything at the end of my shift. Because even after my verbal handover to whoever is going on after me, I have to sit down and run all my dictated reports through the software that copies it to text, then I have another software read it back to me so I can try and catch any errors.

For once, I'm not the only one leaving late. Steve Larabee and I often have shifts together, and I guess you could say we're friends. Tonight, he was unlucky enough to get a rookie taking over his patrol, which made his handover take twice as long. We push open the door to the parking lot together, and I suck in my breath at the freezing air that awaits us.

"Holy fuck, it's cold."

I stuff my hands under my armpits as we hurry out of the police station after finally finishing everything.

Winter has hit Vancouver Island hard this year, and another heavy snowfall started in the last hour. The dark sky is full of the white stuff, making it hard to see, well, anything. There's easily half an inch of snow covering the ground, soft and fluffy.

"No kidding. Damn, this is gonna make shit interesting tomorrow," Steve replies. "You're lucky you're off, Callaghan."

I give him a grin. "Yep, you have fun, Larabee. I'll be making snow angels while you're digging out abandoned cars."

He lets out a groan. "You could always volunteer for overtime."

"Not happening. I'm gonna drink hot chocolate, eat cookies, and watch the snow."

Steve chuckles. "You're something else, Callaghan. Drive safe tonight."

He walks over to his car as I stand at my own, brushing the snow off, and fighting to not take his offhand comment as anything more than just that. Logically, I'm sure he didn't mean it to be an insult, but after a lifetime of feeling different from everyone else — feeling *less than* everyone else — I'm sensitive.

Too fucking sensitive.

Thankfully, the snowstorm means I need to put all my attention on driving home safely. I take it slow, grateful the town has a dedicated snowplow. Thankfully, I don't come across anyone that needs any help, and I make it home in one piece. As I pull into my driveway, I have to grudgingly admit it was a good call to get up extra early and salt everything this morning.

I gather up all my stuff, then dash to my front door as quickly as I can. But when I open my front door, the warmth I'm expecting isn't there.

"What the fuck." I say into the cold quiet of my house. The lights come on, and I can see lights on in other houses on the street. I drop my gear down on the couch; for once in my career, my priority is not locking up my weapons, it's figuring out why my heat isn't on.

I make my way to the back of the kitchen where the furnace and hot water heater are in a small closet. When I rented this house from Ethan Monroe, he told me the furnace was new, some fancy high efficiency thing. But something tells me it isn't working all that efficiently right now.

Sure enough, the sophisticated furnace is cold. Flipping the circuit does nothing. And that's the extent of my knowledge when it comes to home maintenance.

I get out my phone to text Ethan, then pause. It's late, dark, and the roads are covered in snow. It would be dangerous for anyone to head out in this. I'll head back to the station, crash there for the night, then call Ethan tomorrow.

As quickly as I can, I go to my bedroom and pull together a change of clothes and some toiletries. Once that's all in a bag, I turn the faucets on to a trickle in the bathroom and the kitchen, then lock up once again. By now my car is covered in snow, and my tire tracks are invisible.

"Fuck," I swear under my breath, shivering as I do. All I wanted was to go to bed in my warm house. But unless I want to wear six sweaters and pile all my blankets on top of myself and still risk freezing, I've got a night on the rock-hard couch at the station to look forward to.

I'm almost to my car when, in the silence only a heavy snow-fall can bring, I hear a voice, crystal clear.

"Hunter? Is everything okay?"

I look over to see Kat huddled on her porch, some big blanket thing wrapped around her shoulders. Shit, what if her furnace is broken, too?

"Is your furnace working?" I ask, trying to hide the worry.

She nods and tugs the blanket tighter around her. "Yes, it's fine. Why?"

I sag in relief. "Good. That's good." I start to brush off my car, silently telling my heart to slow the fuck down. "Go inside, Kitty Kat. It's too cold to be out here."

"Then tell me why you're out here."

Stubborn woman. I can't avoid the small smile at her saucy reply. "I'm heading back to the station for the night. Furnace is broken and I don't want Ethan or a repair guy coming out."

Kat moves to step down off her porch, then stops; I'm guess-ing because she's not wearing boots. "That's crazy Hunter. You shouldn't drive in this, either."

"Kat," I start, but then stop. What am I meant to say? I just told her I don't want anyone driving in the storm, but I'm going to?

"Come in and sleep here."

My hand freezes, the snow brush halfway across my wind-shield. "What?"

She stamps her feet a few times. "Come on, it's freezing. Get over here."

If I thought my heart was racing before, that's nothing com-pared to what it's doing now. Except this time, it's a very misplaced anticipation. She's offering me a warm place to sleep. That's it.

Down boy, down.

"You sure you're okay with that?" I call over, even as I start to make my way through the heavy drifts of snow, to her house.

"Of course, I am. I trust you, Hunter. And I'm not going to let you freeze." Her tone is final, with no room for me to argue. Not that I want to argue. Fuck no, I just want to get warm.

And a couple of minutes later, my wish is granted when I shut Kat's front door behind me. Letting out a long exhale, I let the warmth seep into me.

"Damn, that feels good." My eyes fly open as soon as the words leave me. Shit, that sounded sexual. Goddamnit. Two minutes and I'm probably already making her uncomfortable. "Sorry, Kat."

I find her standing on the other side of the room, looking at me with open interest in her eyes.

Well, okay then, maybe I didn't say the wrong thing.

"Don't apologize. You must have been freezing." She unwraps the blanket and drops it on the couch, revealing her curves covered in leggings and a loose sweater.

Seeing her here, in her own space, so casual and relaxed, it's another side to Kat and I like it. A lot. Things started to shift between us the other day when she brought over cookies, and it's tempting — really tempting — to move things further along.

But fast on the heels of that thought comes another.

No. Fucking. Way.

Because all around me are pieces of indisputable proof that Kat is not for me. Photos of her with her brothers and parents line the walls. Sawyer's face glares at me from one, I swear. Textbooks are open on the coffee table, highlighted in different colours. There's paper with handwritten notes and a laptop next to an empty mug. More books fill a bookshelf on one wall, interspersed with more photos.

I set my bag down next to the couch and take off my jacket without meeting her curious gaze. "Thanks again for letting me sleep here. It'll be a lot more comfortable than the couch at the station, that's for sure."

"Don't they have beds or something, like the fire department does?"

"Yeah, but that's for the guys on shift. I couldn't take one from them."

Finally, I look at her, and she's got a soft, warm, inviting smile. "You're a good man, Hunter."

My eyes drop to the floor again as I fight back a blush. "Nah."

I hear her move and look up to see her disappearing into the kitchen.

"Want something to drink?" she calls out, and I slowly follow her voice. The kitchen, just like the living room, is a perfect representation of Kat. It's colourful and full of personal touches, but tidy and organized at the same time.

"No, I'm okay. Don't let me keep you up," I say, watching her stifle a yawn.

She gives me a sheepish smile. "Okay. We should both get some sleep. I'm guessing you had a busy shift with the snow."

As she passes by me on the way back to the living room, I get a whiff of that unmistakable tropical scent that will always make me think of her. She opens a closet I hadn't noticed when I first came in and pulls out a big fluffy duvet and a pillowcase. Putting them on the couch, she disappears down the hall, returning a few seconds later with a pillow.

"The couch pulls out into a bed. My brothers have all slept on it at some point, and they say it's pretty comfy. Bathroom is down the hall, just help yourself to whatever you need."

"I'm sure it'll be great." My voice is all gravelly, and her eyes snap up to meet mine. The air is charged. Her lips part, and fucking hell, do I ever want to kiss her.

She lets her breath out on a little puff of an exhale and the tension is broken. Taking a step back, I lift the cushions off the couch, locate the handle, and unfold the bed.

"Okay, well, I guess I'll go to bed. Um, see you in the morning." Her soft words are hesitant, as is my reply.

"Yeah. Thanks, Kat. See you in the morning."

I watch her walk down the hall to what I assume is her bedroom. Once her door shuts, I sink down on the surprisingly comfortable sofa bed and drop my head into my hands.

Knowing she's right down the hall is going to be pure torture.

Maybe I'd have slept better at the station after all.

CHAPTER NINE

Kat

Trying to sleep knowing Hunter is just outside my bedroom door proves to be impossible. I tossed and turned all night, obsessing over whether he could hear me or not.

I roll over in bed and fumble to turn off my alarm. My body feels twitchy and agitated, and it takes me a minute to realize it's because I'm horny. Then I'm grabbing my pillow and using it to stifle a groan of embarrassment. My dreams come back to me in flashes — naked, writhing on the sheets, moaning his name.

Oh God, I hope I didn't say anything out loud.

Maybe I'll just stay in here until he eventually leaves. But how will I know when he leaves? What if he already snuck out because he heard me moaning out his name like a hussy! *Crap,* I'll never live this down.

The sound of a toilet flushing and then the bathroom door opening and closing springs me into action. I jump out of bed, throw my hair up in a messy bun, and ignore the dark circles under my eyes. Pulling a hoodie over my tank top, I carefully open the door to my bedroom. The hallway is empty, so I dart across it into the bathroom to brush my teeth and splash some cold water on my face.

Staring at myself in the mirror, I try to get a grip on things. I have to face him eventually.

I open the door slowly and walk down the hall. My eyes go immediately to the couch, but to my surprise, the bed has already been put away, the duvet and pillow folded neatly on top. Sounds come from the kitchen, and I pivot to see Hunter opening and closing cabinets. The bag of coffee beans is out on the counter beside him, and like one of Pavlov's dogs, my mouth starts to water.

"Look to the right of the fridge," I say as I enter the kitchen. He twists and gives me a grin over his shoulder before moving to the correct cabinet and taking down two mugs.

"Morning, Kitty Kat."

He fills the mugs with coffee, then reaches into my fridge and pulls out my special holiday creamer. The entire thing feels weird. But like, a good weird. A domestic, intimate weird.

After pouring some peppermint mocha creamer into a mug and stirring it, he hands it to me. "I don't know if you want sugar, but I assume you like this stuff since there's two bottles in your fridge."

I swallow my first sip of rich, fresh coffee and sigh happily. "Thank you. This is perfect."

Hunter eyes his mug speculatively before shrugging and pouring some creamer into his own. He lifts the mug to his mouth, and my eyes follow, watching shamelessly as he takes a drink. His Adam's apple moves as he swallows, and I squeeze my legs together automatically.

Seriously? The way he swallows turns me on? Good grief, I

think I need a session with my vibrator tonight to take the edge off or something. This is ridiculous.

"Huh, that's actually pretty freaking good," he comments, giving me a wide smile over his mug. "Peppermint mocha creamer. Who would've guessed I'd like that."

"It's Christmas in a mug," I say, taking another drink. "Who *wouldn't* like that."

"The grinch," he answers seriously. I stare at him, and a beat later he chuckles, and I join him.

"You have a great laugh in the morning."

I almost choke on my sip of coffee at his oddly specific comment. "Only in the morning?"

Hunter blushes, and it's the cutest thing ever. And yet, I'm starting to notice a pattern. Any time he says something funny, or teasing, it's as if he instantly second-guesses himself. Like he regrets it or is worried I'll be upset. Which is the farthest thing from the truth. All I want to do is wrap my arms around him, hold on tight, and soak up some of his goodness.

"I don't know why I said that."

I clear my throat and give him a big smile. "You're taken by my deep morning voice, I get it. It's irresistible. Like Sam Elliott and James Earl Jones had a baby."

Hunter almost chokes on his coffee with laughter. "Oh, fuck no."

"C'mon, lets go sit in the living room." I move out of the kitchen, determined to keep that smile on his face. For some reason, I occasionally get the feeling that Hunter doesn't think as highly of himself as I know so many other people do. Does he really think his happy, funny nature is not a good thing?

Is that sense of humour masking something else?

We sit down on opposite ends of the couch and drink our coffee in silence. Once again, I'm struck by how relaxed and comfortable it is being with him in my house. I don't remember it ever being this easy even having Tyson at my house.

"I have to say, I expected you to have a house full of Christmas gnomes or something," Hunter says with a wink. "But instead, nothing. Not a candy cane in sight."

"It's the first week of December and I just finished exams. Cut me some slack." I narrow my eyes back at him. "Besides, I don't recall seeing any Christmas lights at your house, either."

"That's because I still need to buy some decorations."

"I could always use another gnome," I quip. "Want to hit the stores together? I'll leave Sawyer at home this time."

Hunter's entire face shutters for the briefest of seconds, then it clears. But the smile he gives me doesn't quite reach his eyes, and he won't meet my gaze.

"Sure, yeah, I'm not exactly certain when I'll have time, but hey, that could be fun."

If ever there was a brush-off, that was it. With one stupid suggestion to go shopping together, I've managed to make things awkward. And succeeded in having my confidence in the idea of Hunter being interested in me thoroughly shaken.

"No worries. It was just an idea." I stand up from the couch and brush an invisible piece of lint from my leg. "I'm gonna go get dressed. No rush on getting out of here, though, stay in the warm as long as you want."

I don't even bother stopping in the kitchen to drop off my mug, instead beelining straight to my bedroom to hide out.

Flopping down on my bed, I bury my face in my pillow and silently scream in frustration.

I honestly didn't think I was reading things so wrong. I thought Hunter was maybe interested in starting something with me. But now, I don't know what to think.

I've asked him to the gala, I've brought him cookies, and I just asked if he wanted to go shopping with me. Okay, none of those necessarily scream *let's have sex*, but wasn't I at least clear in communicating I want to be more than just his friendly neighbour?

After a few more minutes wallowing in a stupid pool of self-pity, I drag myself up and get dressed. When I come back out of my bedroom, I find Hunter standing by the couch, holding his phone in his hand, and looking like he doesn't know what to do next.

"I just talked to Ethan; he's sending a repair guy out to look at my furnace now. Thanks again for letting me crash here."

I give what I hope is an encouraging smile, even though a part of me wishes that weren't the case, and I could have a reason to ask him to stay another night. "That's great. Hopefully your pipes are all good, too."

"I turned them on last night."

The stilted small talk sucks. I hate it, and it's not like us. I just wish I could go back in time and not say anything about going shopping together. But how was I to know an innocent suggestion would make him pull away? Although...was it the shopping or was it mentioning Sawyer? God, my freaking brother is managing to ruin my chances at a dating life even when he isn't anywhere near me. Just as I'm resigning myself to saying goodbye to Hunter and leaving things all weird between us, he draws himself up straight and looks me directly in the eye.

"Kat, I want to take you out. On a date. A real date."

My heart stutters a beat as my eyebrows lift so high they might as well fly off my face. "A date?"

He nods. "Yeah. A date. Where I pick you up, take you out, we have a nice time, and if I'm lucky, you let me kiss you at the end of it."

Hunter wants to kiss me. My tongue darts out to moisten my lips, and his eyes zero in on the motion.

Oh. My. God.

"What d'you say, Kitty Kat? Will you go out on a date with me?"

CHAPTER TEN

Hunter

"Dude, she's not a dirty little secret, just take her anywhere."
Asher shoves a handful of chips in his mouth.

"It's not that simple," I grunt, my eyes slowly reading the
reviews in front of me for some restaurant. I've been doing this
for over an hour now, trying to figure out where to take Kat on
our date. It can't be anywhere local, that's one thing. "She just
got out of a relationship, her cousin is my boss, and her brothers
basically run this town. And I'm not exactly ready for them to
know I'm taking her out."

"Dunno why not, like I've said before, you're a catch," he
says, teasing. Nonetheless, I glare at him. He just shrugs. "Fine,
fine. I'll leave you to your delusions of not being worthy. Why
don't you just cook for her?"

"I thought about that, but is it good enough for a first date?"

Asher raises an eyebrow. "Hunter, you're a fucking amazing
cook. Yes, it would be good enough."

Even though he's complimenting me, I can't focus on that
right now. "Yeah, yeah, I can make decent food. But dinner
at my house, isn't that, I dunno, too personal? Or too cheap?

What if she thinks I'm cooking because I can't afford to take her out?"

Asher holds up his hand. "Holy hell, calm down. I know you're nervous, but breathe, my brother, breathe. Listen. Instead of obsessing over restaurant reviews, why don't you let me help. My buddy Nico's family owns Grecian Steak House. He'll set up a romantic night if you want; he hooked me up when I was dating Lucy. She went gaga over it all."

Relief floods me. "Seriously? Dude, that's fucking perfect. Why the hell didn't you suggest that earlier?"

The asshole has the decency to look sheepish. "Sorry." Then he taps out something on his phone, and less than a minute later, looks back at me. "Done. You have a reservation for seven tonight. You're welcome."

"I would say I owe you, but I'm pretty sure you just finished all the beer I had in my apartment," I reply drily. Asher shrugs his shoulders, then stands up and scratches his stomach.

"Yeah, I'll bring some over next time. Anyway, now that I've played fairy godfather for your date, I'm out. Have fun tonight, be safe."

Once Ash leaves, I send a quick message to Kat, telling her what time I'll pick her up.

Now all that's left to do is figure out how to keep my brain occupied. I need to pass the next several hours before my date without massively overthinking and panicking about going out with the woman I've had a crush on for so long.

No sweat.

Standing on Kat's front porch a few hours later, I rub my hands on my jeans frantically, hoping they aren't too clammy.

When she steps out the door and gives me a small smile, I realize there's nothing that could have prepared me for this moment.

Kat Donnelly is beautiful all the time.

But wearing dark jeans that look like they're made for her curves, a cream-coloured sweater that drapes down, baring one shoulder, and makeup that only intensifies the green colour of her eyes and the glow to her skin? Kat has stolen the breath from my body. My brain no longer knows how to formulate words.

She is stunning.

"Hi."

I blink and realize while my brain short-circuited from her beauty, she put her coat on and is now standing next to me.

"Hi. Sorry. I, um. Yeah. I should've helped you with your coat or something," I stutter, still trying to get my fucking head to clear.

"It's fine, Hunter." Her brow furrows slightly. "Is everything okay, though? You look distracted."

"You're so fucking beautiful," I blurt out. "Shit. That was meant to be my inside voice. Not that it isn't true, I mean, I just didn't plan on saying it like that. Fuck. I need to stop talking now." That last sentence I mumble to myself, certain I'm screwing this date up before it even has a chance to start.

But then, Kat's hand finds its way to tangle with mine.

"Thank you."

She licks her lips, and it's everything I can do not to lean in and kiss her right here, right now. We haven't even started our date and I'm already desperate to reach the end of it so I can make good on the promise I made to her yesterday.

Because yet again, with a handful of words and one touch of her hand, Kat has erased my nerves and made me feel like the luckiest guy on the fucking planet.

When I open the door for her, she looks up at me with a smile. "Such a gentleman," she teases as she slides into her seat.

Defaulting to my regular charm and humour to try and cover up the bumbling idiot I've been thus far, I lean in slightly. "You know what they say about gentlemen," I say with a waggle of my eyebrows.

"What?" she asks.

I drop my voice down low, hoping for an over-the-top seductive tone. "Gentleman in the streets, bad boy in the sheets."

Her laughter fills the air as I go around to the driver's side, climb in, and buckle up. Mission accomplished — Kat's smiling, and I've got some sliver of control over myself.

"Are you planning on being a bad boy or a gentleman tonight?" Kat asks coyly and my hands grip the steering wheel tightly, so I don't do something stupid, like touch her. I shift in my seat to face her and the attraction I'm positive is written all over my damn face is reflected back at me.

Holy hell. She wants this, too. I school my reaction before giving her a subtle wink.

"Gentleman, of course. You deserve nothing less for our *first* date."

Dinner starts out fine. We laugh over calamari and share child-hood stories over souvlaki.

Then it's time for dessert.

"I'm so full, but I absolutely love baklava. Want to share one with me?" The smile on Kat's face would make me say yes to anything, even if I am totally stuffed.

"Sure."

"Do you mind ordering while I just go..." She nods her head toward the bathroom, and I nod hurriedly.

"Of course. No problem."

Except when the waiter comes to take our order, I realize I can't remember what she said. Bah something?

It gets worse when I open the dessert menu and the page swims with unfamiliar Greek words. In the dim light, it's even harder to read. The waiter's looking at me expectantly and my chest is tightening with the pressure. I point blindly at some-thing that starts with a "b" and hope I guessed right.

But when it arrives, Kat looks at it quizzically. "That's an odd-looking baklava. Interesting." She picks up a bite on her fork and some sort of creamy filling oozes out. She makes a face and my heart plummets. "Oh, that's not baklava, that's why."

Shitfuckdamnit. I must have pointed to the wrong thing on the menu. Fuck. I should have listened closer to what she said, so I could've just said it back to the waiter. I'm such a screwup.

"Fuck. It's my fault, I couldn't remember what you said. I'm so sorry. I'll get them back and order the right one."

"No, it's okay, Hunter. We don't need dessert. No big deal."

"It is a big deal. I screwed up." I start looking around for the waiter, determined to make this right.

"Hunter, stop."

There's a firmness in her voice that leaves no room for argument. I slowly turn to face her.

"It's just dessert. You didn't screw anything up." The warmth in her quiet words washes over me, replacing my self-criticism with relief.

I lean back in my chair and run my hand through my hair. How does she manage to put me at ease better than anyone else in my life ever has? She has no idea that just by being her, she builds me up and makes me feel like a better man.

"I just want tonight to be perfect for you," I say, letting a bit of vulnerability show.

Kat lays her hand out on the table, palm up, and I cover it with my own. That simple touch grounds me and connects us.

"Perfect is overrated. I'm having a good time, Hunter. The food was delicious, and the company is wonderful. It's the best date I've been on in a really, *really* long time. The wrong dessert doesn't change any of that, so stop apologizing."

I sigh deeply and smile sheepishly at her. "Sorry." I wince and she laughs lightly. "Damn it, you know what I mean. I'm just nervous." I blow out a huff of air. "At the risk of sounding like a sap, I've wanted to go out with you for a really long time."

"But I was with Tyson," she says quietly, dropping her eyes to the table.

I reach over, and gently tip her chin up. "Yeah, you were, but you're not now."

Her smile returns, thank fuck. There's a hint of the pain I'm guessing she still feels about her asshole ex cheating on her, but the warmth and happiness is back.

"If we aren't getting dessert, should we get out of here? Maybe go for a walk?"

Kat nods, and the last trace of pain vanishes from her face. "That sounds lovely."

I pay the bill, and soon we're walking along the waterfront of Westport. Kat slips her hand in mine, and I swear, my heart grows impossibly large inside of my chest.

She makes me feel like I could conquer the world.

"My brother Max lives in Westport, to be close to the hospital he works at. I like it here, but honestly, give me the small-town energy of Dogwood Cove over this hustle and bustle any day."

Her offhand comment is like a bucket of ice being dumped over my head. Because with just one reminder of her brothers, I'm faced with the reality that eventually, they're going to find out Kat and I went out on a date.

And there's no fucking way they'll ever think this is a good idea. That *I'm* a good idea.

Tightening my grip on Kat's hand, I try to push that thought aside, at least for now. I'm on a date with the woman of my dreams, and I just want to enjoy it. Especially if it ends up being the only one I get with her once the other Donnellys find out.

To my surprise, I manage to compartmentalize my panic and worry just enough to enjoy the rest of my walk with Kat and the drive home.

The date went by way too quickly. And now we're standing outside Kat's house, and I'm mentally debating whether to risk being seen kissing her. I desperately want to. But what if someone drives past?

But her thumb is slowly stroking across my knuckles, and

she's looking up at me as if I hung the moon and stars. Which I definitely did not. My body starts to move on its own, the decision about kissing her clearly made.

I move slowly, in case she's not ready for this, but then I see the small intake of breath and her pupils dilate. That's all the proof I need.

As soon as I lean down and cover her lips with mine, I'm a goner. My tongue teases the seam of her mouth, and she opens easily. I take it deeper. There's no resistance; Kat is into this kiss just as much as I am, and that thought makes me soar.

Her hands slide down my back until they're hovering just above my hips. I tighten my grip on the back of her neck, just slightly, and angle her head so I can rain kisses down the smooth slope of her throat.

"Hunter," she says breathily, and I feel her fingers dig into my back just above the waistline of my jeans.

I make my way back up to her lips and press another deep kiss there. I could do this forever. But I manage to find the strength and self-control to pull back, kissing her lightly on the nose before sliding my hands down and tangling them with hers.

"Thank you for an amazing time, Kitty Kat."

She lets out a breathy laugh. "Pretty sure I should be thanking you." She squeezes my hands and licks her lips seductively. "I wish tonight didn't have to end."

"Kat," I groan. "Remember what I said earlier? I'm trying to be a gentleman."

She rises on her toes and brings her mouth to my ear. "I don't always want a gentleman. Sometimes I want a bad boy who's willing to break the rules." She drops back down and winks.

"But you're right. We should be good. Save something for the second date."

She's already thinking of a second date. Somehow, I didn't fuck everything up. Holy shit. "That second date is happening really soon, right?" I ask, caught up in the moment and the tremulous hope that I might actually get a second date with her.

"Sounds good to me."

We stand there holding hands, grinning like fools for a moment before I finally step away from her warmth.

"Night, Kitty Kat," I reply, pushing my hands into my coat pockets to try and arrange the cover to hide the bulge in my pants. Except all that does is draw attention to it, given how Kat's eyes drop down, then back up to me with a flare of heat.

"Goodnight, Hunter." Kat takes a step back, a saucy smile covering her beautiful face. She turns and opens her door, gives me one more smile over her shoulder, and then closes it.

It's only when I'm inside my own house that I let out a long, slow exhale. The date had its moments, but overall, it went better than I possibly could have expected. Only now, there's a whole new set of things for me to freak out about.

Because I've had a taste of Kat Donnelly. And with that one taste, I'm addicted.

Even if I'm not good enough for her.

Even if her brothers try to push me away.

There's no turning back now.

Chapter Eleven

Kat

"Someone's looking pretty happy for a Thursday morning. Doesn't she look happy, Mila?" Serena smirks at me over her travel mug. Now that she's with my cousin, she's family to me as well. Including all the nosy teasing, apparently.

"Exams are over. I'm excited for the break," I answer hurriedly, tying my apron around my waist.

I forgot how damn perceptive the women around here are.

Serena eyes me critically. "Hmm. Okay, fine. I don't buy that for a second, but I also don't have time to push for the truth. I'm outta here, ladies, there are precious young minds to teach."

With a flourish, she turns and leaves, but it's Mila's turn to stare, a knowing smile on her face. "She's not wrong, you know. You do seem to have a glow about you today. Are you sure it's just winter break that has you feeling so good?"

I nod, trying not to be too obvious. Hunter and I didn't exactly get the chance to talk last night about how to tell people we're dating, if that's even what we're calling it. He did seem excited about the idea of a second date, but I can't help still feeling a bit apprehensive.

Just because I can see myself falling for him hard and fast doesn't mean he feels the same way.

"Yup, totally just winter break. Can't wait to sleep in, maybe read a book that isn't for school, you know?"

Does my voice sound too cheery? Ugh. I don't know. Mila still has her eagle eyes on me. The damn woman is a super sleuth. But I'm saved from further interrogation by someone calling her name from the bakery side of the building.

Just as she walks away, the door opens and my cousin walks in, giving me a wave.

"Hey, Leo, you just missed Serena." I put a coffee cup on the counter in front of him and fill it with the last of the pot.

"I saw her on my way in." The content expression on his face makes my heart pang. In the year and a half since Leo and his daughter moved to Dogwood Cove, I've never seen two people more in love. They found each other after almost two decades apart, and their second chance at love has been the start of forever together.

I want that someday.

"That's good. How's work? Everything going okay? Any big crime sprees?" Here's hoping Leo isn't as good of a detective as he probably should be, or he'll see right through my not-so-subtle question. I've never bothered to ask him about work before, that's for sure. And the only reason I am now is because I'm desperate for any hint of how Hunter's doing today.

But he doesn't question me; instead, Leo's brows draw together. "No crime sprees. Everything's fine."

"That didn't sound convincing."

"You're too observant sometimes. Maybe you should forget

the nurse practitioner gig and become a cop." He says it lightly, teasing, but then Leo falls silent and takes a sip of his coffee, studying me. "You know some of the guys from the station pretty well, don't you?"

I grab a cloth and start wiping at an imaginary spot on the counter, resolutely avoiding his eyes. "I mean, yeah, I guess so."

"Well, if you ever get a chance to find out why one of them decided not to put his name in for the next round of promotions, that would be a good thing. Because I must admit, I was disappointed I didn't see a certain name on the list."

I stare at him. "Hunter?" I blurt out, not thinking about the fact I just obliterated any chance of Leo not figuring out I'm involved with him somehow.

"I can't tell you that, Kat. But if the hunch I've had about you two for quite a while now is correct, maybe you can get through to him. He needs to stop holding himself back."

Leo stands up casually, as if he hasn't just dropped a couple of bombs in my lap. "I gotta get back to work. Think about what I said, Kat." He raps the counter, staring straight in my eyes. "And what I didn't say." He walks out with a backward wave, leaving me lost in thought.

Then, before I can dwell anymore on what Leo just told me, the door opens again, and my mom comes in with the rest of The Walkie Talkies. I give them a wave before starting to fill enough cups of coffee for all of them.

Carrying over the tray, I set it down and smile hello to the other women seated around the table. Sometimes Hattie Henderson joins them, but not today. Today it's just Mom, Lily's mother Barbara, and Sandra, whose husband Turner owns the hardware store. Just as Sandra's asking me about how I think my exams went, Hunter himself walks in with a couple other cops. Immediately my eyes fall on him, and I mumble some sort of reply to Sandra and walk back to the counter to fill more coffee cups. I can already feel a stupidly large smile stretch across my face just from seeing him. But when I approach, Hunter doesn't even look at me as he turns and drops into a chair, deep in conversation with his coworkers.

Weird.

Making my way over to the table, I greet the other officers first, taking their orders with a smile. When I get to Hunter, I try to act casual as I shift my body toward him, letting my hip brush against his side.

"What can I get you, Hunter?" My voice is a little more flirty than usual, but that's okay, right? We can flirt now, can't we? I mean, the man had his tongue down my throat last night.

Except Hunter doesn't react like it's okay.

No. He actually shifts *away* from me and doesn't even look up when he answers. "Coffee and a breakfast sandwich. Thanks, Kat."

I stand there frozen, my mouth open for a second or two before snapping myself out of it. "Right. Got it."

Keep it together. Just keep it together. I chant to myself, blinking away the confusion and hurt that's building, thanks to how he just responded to me. Dropping the order off, I mumble to one of my coworkers I just need a minute. Then I hustle back to the staff room which is, thankfully, empty.

I close the door and sink down onto one of the chairs. What the actual heck just happened? Did he really just give me the cold shoulder? All my fears come rushing up to meet me as I try to take in a full breath.

But then the door to the staff room flies open and Hunter drops down to his knees in front of me, his hands coming to the arms of the chair.

"Kitty Kat, I'm so sorry. Fuck. I didn't know how to act or what to do, and we haven't told anyone, and I was a total shithead to you, and I'm so sorry." He drops his head to look at the floor.

When he looks back up, the guilt I see etched on his face destroys me. This vulnerable side he showed briefly last night is making me realize the happy-go-lucky man everyone else sees, that I used to see, might be covering something else up.

"What was that out there?"

He lets out a long sigh, finally taking my hands in his. "That was me being a goddamn coward. It's just, we never talked about telling people we went out last night, and I guess I figured if we decided this was real for us, I'd talk to Leo and let him know first. Y'know, as my boss and your cousin."

"Is it real for you?" I ask quietly, terrified and eager to know his answer.

His tongue darts out and moistens his lips. Then slowly, he nods.

A small relieved smile creases my face. "It's real for me, too. Which means I want to tell people we're dating. I want to be able to kiss you hello."

Hunter's eyes darken and he leans in.

"I want that, too."

I put my hand against his chest. "But you're right."

He jerks back in surprise.

"We do need to talk to my family before we go public, so they know to back the heck off and let me live my own life."

A flash of worry crosses his face, but it's gone before I can even think enough about it to question him.

When Hunter picks me up the next day for a snowshoe hike, it's a very different situation.

As soon as I walk out of my front door, he runs up to me, swinging me up into the air and crushing me into his body.

"Hi," he mumbles, the word muffled, given his face is crammed into the collar of my winter coat.

"Hi." I giggle in return, swatting feebly at his shoulder. "Put me down, please?"

He slowly lowers me to the ground, then cups my face and kisses me deeply. When he finally lets go, we're both breathing heavily. "That's how I wanted to say hi to you yesterday."

"Uh-huh," I say, still a little dazed from the intensity of his kiss. Hunter laughs and pushes me toward his car, slapping my butt gently as we go.

"Maybe it's a good thing I didn't. How could you possibly handle serving all of Dogwood Cove the food they so desperately want if you're reduced to a pile of goo from one kiss." His cocky, teasing tone is so full of light and joy; it's the exact opposite of the scared, vulnerable man from yesterday. The two sides of him are dizzying and I need to make sense of it, sooner rather than later.

"I am not goo, thank you very much," I reply, then immediately slip on a patch of ice. Hunter catches me with a chuckle and tucks me into his side.

"Sure, Kitty Kat. Sure."

An hour or so later, we're in a half-empty parking lot at the top of Mount Washington, strapping our boots into snowshoes. It's a perfect winter day — the skies are clear, the snow is sparkling, and it's crisp, but without any cold wind.

Hand in hand, we take off down a trail, just barely wide enough for two people. Hunter has to forge his own path sometimes, but it's worth it. His smile is back, dazzlingly bright, and the energy between us is full of happiness.

When we reach the lookout where a bench has been recently cleared of snow, we take off our snowshoes and sit down close enough our thighs are touching. I shiver slightly as a cold wind passes through, and Hunter wraps his arm around my shoulders and tugs me in even closer. My eyes fall shut and I breathe in the moment.

"What made you ask me to the gala?"

My eyes pop open as heat floods my cheeks at his seemingly out of nowhere question. But I suppose he's allowed to wonder. We did go a long time securely in the just-barely-friends-more-like-acquaintances-who-happen-to-be-neighbors zone.

"Honestly, the answer isn't all that exciting," I start, trying to downplay it. "Lily was giving me a hard time about needing to move on after my ex. She knew I liked you, so she dared me to ask you to the gala, knowing I can't say no to dares."

Hunter laughs. "Now this, I gotta hear. You can't say no to a dare?"

I give him a sheepish smile. "You try growing up with four older brothers. I just wanted to do whatever they were doing, but sometimes I was scared. Jude figured out those three words, 'I dare you,' were the key to get me to do whatever I was scared of."

"That's awesome. You conquer your fears, instead of letting them hold you back." There's a wistful note to his voice, but it's gone as quickly as it appeared. "I'll have to remember those three words." He gives me a playful wink.

I narrow my eyes. "If you try to use that against me, you'll be in big trouble, mister."

He lifts my hands to his, pressing a kiss to them, all the while keeping an impish grin on his face. "No promises, Kitty Kat. But I guess I do need to thank Lily for knowing how to get you to act."

I lift my chin. "Okay, fair's fair. That's why I asked you to the gala. What made you ask me on a date?"

His handsome face softens, the mischievous smile melting into something far more romantic. "Truthfully, you did. I could tell you were nervous, asking me to the gala. But you did it anyway. And I managed to convince myself to just go for it by rationalizing that you wouldn't have asked me if you didn't feel *something* for me. I figured even if you just meant us to go to the gala as friends, me asking you to dinner wasn't that big of a stretch."

"Well, I'm really glad you did."

"Me too."

We both fall silent, staring at each other with what I'm sure are dumb, swoony looks on our faces.

"I wish we hadn't wasted so much time with both of us being nervous."

Hunter's head ducks down at my quiet statement. He's staring at his hands. "Yeah, me too. If I had just…"

He trails off. But there's no way I can handle not knowing what he was about to say. "If you had just what?"

His eyes raise to meet mine again. "If I had just asked you out when I first met you, like I wanted to. Then we wouldn't have wasted so much time."

"I was with Tyson," I say lamely, but it's a weak excuse. A half-hearted attempt at protecting my heart from falling for Hunter even more.

"Not when I first moved in next door, you weren't."

There it is. The confession that makes me simultaneously thrilled and scared. The fact that Hunter has harboured secret feelings for me for as long as I have for him should make me feel better about finally moving forward with him. But what if, now that it's out in the open, now that we've taken this first step, he realizes those feelings aren't all he thought they were after all?

A somber quiet descends once again. I know this conversation is important, but I can't help wishing for Hunter to turn on his magnetic charm and bring some lightness back. Because the longer things stay heavy and emotionally charged, the more the walls around my heart start coming down, and the pull I feel toward him grows more and more intense.

As if he read my mind, Hunter reaches into his backpack, pulling out a thermos and two mugs. "What do you say we raise a cup of hot chocolate to Lily's dare, starting the chain reaction that led to this moment. After all, if she hadn't challenged you, who knows how long we'd have suffered as neighbors, pining over each other, never knowing the feelings were mutual." The mock horror in his voice breaks the tension exactly the way I hoped he would.

I giggle, taking the mug when he hands it to me. "You know, Lily didn't just dare me to ask you to the gala," I say, eyeing Hunter over the top of my mug.

He narrows his eyes. "Really. What else did she dare you to do?"

I lift my shoulders in a slight shrug. "If I remember right, she mentioned something about finally getting some much-needed orgasms."

"Huh. I see. And she was hoping I'd be the one to give those to you, I assume?" he says all too casually.

My body starts to heat up. I tug my lower lip between my teeth. "Mm-hmm."

My only warning is a low growl before Hunter lunges at me, knocking my mug out of the way and tackling me to the snowy ground. Hot chocolate spills out over the snow, and I let out a shriek as he somehow manages it so we land with him underneath me, his hands going straight to my ass, pulling me tight against him.

"You have no idea what it does to me hearing you talk about orgasms, Kitty Kat. If I wasn't worried about freezing certain body parts, I'd take care of that for you right now."

I drop my head down, closing the small gap between us, and nip at his lip before kissing him. "Then tell me why, exactly, we're lying in the cold snow *talking* about orgasms when we could be on our way home now to *have* orgasms?"

He tilts his head to the side, the movement so similar to what a dog would do when faced with a delicious treat. I can't help but laugh again. "Good point."

Then Hunter rolls me off him, bounces to his feet, and drags me up to stand, straight into his arms. "Let's go."

We move over to the bench, and I start picking up my water bottle and gloves.

"Hurry up, woman," he commands, and I look over to see him frantically shoving things into his backpack. He turns to me with a mock glower. "We need to get back down the mountain, Kitty Kat, or it won't matter how cold the snow is, you'll be getting those orgasms right here."

CHAPTER TWELVE

Hunter

I won't lie and say I didn't break some speed limits getting us home, but I still drove carefully, mindful of my precious cargo in the passenger seat.

Part of me can't believe this is happening. Kat wanting to have sex with me. But a deeper, darker, more primal side of me is slowly taking over, telling me to claim her, show her she's mine, and never let her go. Because I've never been with someone who makes me feel so good. Like I could maybe do anything, like I'm not the *never going to amount to anything important* man I've believed I was for so long.

As soon as my car is parked in my driveway, I'm out and striding around to her door, yanking it open so hard it almost bounces back on me. "Let's go, Kitty Kat," I say gruffly, reaching my hand in and taking hers. Leaving all our bags, jackets, and snowshoes in the trunk, we walk as quickly as possible over to her front door. When she starts to fumble with her key, I hold my hand out silently. She passes it to me and somehow, I manage to get the door open.

Lust takes over the second the door closes behind us. Our

boots are kicked over to the side as I grab her and cover her mouth with mine. Our tongues dance together, thrusting against each other, mimicking what our bodies will do later.

When we pull apart to take a much-needed breath, my eyes travel from Kat's flushed cheeks down to her sweater-covered chest.

"Clothes. Off."

Her eyes darken and as soon as her sweater is off, I can see her nipples pebbling under the thin fabric of her bra. I reach around and unclip it, and she lets it fall to the floor.

Fuck. Me. Her tits are even better than I imagined. Round globes of perfection.

"What about you?" she asks, her hands coming to toy with the bottom of my hoodie. "There are far too many layers of fabric between us right now."

I let her peel my sweater up and over my head, taking my base layer shirt with it. And her reaction to seeing my bare torso for the first time? Makes all those gym sessions worth it.

"Hunter," she hums appreciatively, her fingers running lightly through the hairs on my chest. I bring my hands around to rest on her lower back, just above the ass I've stared at too many times to count. Then she leans in and her tongue darts out to flick my nipple.

"Fuck," I gasp. Just like that, she's trying to flip the script on who's leading this, and that's not gonna happen. Spinning her around, I bring her back to my front. "You'll get your turn, babe, but right now I have so many dirty fantasies I want to live out with you."

Out of the corner of my eye, I spot a full-length mirror.

Perfect.

As I gently guide her in that direction, my fingers move quickly over the fastener at the top of her snow pants. Pushing them down, revealing her tight fleece leggings, I curse inwardly. There really are too many layers between us. Fucking snow gear is slowing me down.

I'm a greedy, impatient bastard and I need her naked. Now.

I push at the hem of her leggings. "These need to go." She gives a murmur of agreement and shimmies her hips as she wiggles them down, pressing that delectable ass right into my crotch as she does so. Then, standing up again, her hands come up and behind her head to twine around my neck.

"Show me those fantasies, Hunter. Let's see if they're the same as mine."

"I want to make all your fantasies come true, babe," I growl in her ear.

I turn us slowly, taking in her audible gasp when she sees we're in front of the mirror and letting it fuel my arousal. Fuck, she's gorgeous. Her nipples are standing straight up, helped by the arch in her back as her fingers dig into my hair. My hands run up the sides of her thighs, squeezing her hips, before sliding around to her stomach. I duck my head down and make my way down her neck, and along her collarbone with my lips.

"You're perfect. The most beautiful woman I've ever seen. I'm gonna make you feel so goddamn good."

"You already do," she whispers, her fingers tightening in my hair as my hands cup her breasts. I squeeze gently, toying with them, playing with her nipples. I listen to her sounds, complete-ly tuned in to every minute movement of her body. It doesn't take long until she's writhing in front of me, just from my lips on her neck, my hands on her tits, and my dirty words in her ear.

"I can't wait to taste your pussy. I bet you taste so fucking sweet. Everything about you is sweet, Kitty Kat. Your heart, your soul, your body. You're everything I've ever wanted, you know that? I can't wait to watch you explode with pleasure."

"Hunter," she moans, thrusting her tits into my hands. "Please."

"Mmm. I like hearing you beg, babe."

"Oh God," she cries out as I dance my fingers lightly over the neatly trimmed hair covering her sex. I want to devour her, but first, she needs to see something.

"Open your eyes, Kat. Watch me. Watch us."

Her eyes fly open and only then do I plunge my fingers into her pussy. She's soaked, throbbing, open and ready for me. Fuck. My dick is aching in my pants, desperate to get out and replace my fingers. But not yet.

Kat moans and pants out my name as one of my arms slides around her to hold her against me, and the other does wicked things between her thighs. I alternate between plucking at her clit and thrusting in and out, watching her, learning her body. If I could, I would dedicate my life to learning Kat's body. To worshipping Kat's body.

When I feel her walls start to tighten around my fingers and hear her voice take on a keening quality, my forehead drops to her shoulder.

I'm in heaven. Getting her off, bringing her pleasure, this is fucking heaven.

"Oh God, Hunter. Oh my God. Yes, oh fuck, yes!"

My eyes dart up and I find her staring at us in the mirror, her own eyes dark and wide with passion. I lock onto that gaze and add a third finger, crooking them slightly. Then, to send her flying, my other hand moves down to roll her clit between my finger and thumb.

"Show me how you explode, Kat."

Kat's hands come to my forearms, which are tightly banded around her body, and she squeezes tightly as her entire body convulses in the most consuming orgasm I have ever witnessed. I hold her, stroking gently over her body until she relaxes in my arms.

I slowly lift my hand up to my mouth, keeping constant eye contact. There's something so fucking hot about watching her, watching me. I lick my fingers that were just inside of her, and I swear as my tongue darts out, Kat's entire body shivers.

"Just like I thought. Sweet."

Kat takes a step forward and slowly pivots to face me. Her eyes drop down to my pants and my cock that is obviously trying to force its way out. "You're still wearing too many clothes."

I tilt my head to the side and give her a wicked grin. "What are you gonna do about that?"

She lifts one eyebrow, and her lips slowly turn up into that gorgeously seductive smile. Then her fingers find their way to my belt loops, and she starts to walk backward, pulling me along with her.

We reach her bedroom, lit only by a small lamp on her bedside table. She steps back into the circle of my arms, but her hands stay between us, making quick work of undoing the button and zipper on my pants.

"This is what I'm going to do. I'm going to take your pants off and hope you've got a condom because mine are so old I wouldn't trust them. Then I'm going to get on that bed and you're going to fuck me with what I'm guessing is one delicious cock you're hiding in here."

"Jesus Christ," I growl as she yanks down my pants so fast it sends a bolt of pain to my rock-hard dick. "Do you have any fucking idea how hot it is hearing you talk like that? Goddamn, woman."

Kat's devilish smile is in full force as she steps backward, then sits down on the edge of her bed in all her gorgeous nude glory. She crooks a finger at me. "Show me how hot."

I bend down and grab the condom I did, thankfully, put in my pocket earlier. Tearing the packet open with my teeth, I roll it on, watching the way she stares greedily, openly at me.

I'm on top of the fucking world right now. And it's all because of this woman.

I stalk over to the bed and lift Kat under her armpits, basically tossing her up to the top of the bed before crawling over her. My fingers dip down and stroke her wet pussy gently. "Mmm. Soaked. You like it dirty, don't you? Watching what I did to you earlier got you so fucking wet. Gotta say, Kitty Kat, I didn't expect that, but it's a really fucking good surprise."

"Hunter," she whimpers as I slide one finger in and out slowly. She doesn't need any more priming; she's so ready for me. "Please."

"I've got you, Kitty Kat."

I line up my cock with her entrance, her legs falling apart and her hands coming up to tangle in my hair again. I lean down to kiss her hungrily, desperate for every bit of connection possible at the exact same time I slide into her wet heat.

Fucking hell. This feels even better than I ever could have imagined. I pull out slightly, then plunge back in, again and again, deeper every time until I'm fully inside of her. Kat's muscles tense around me as her hips start to match my rhythm.

My self-control is barely there, hanging on by a thread as Kat's fingers dig into my shoulders and her heels find their home around my waist.

"Fuck, Hunter. Oh God."

"Jesus, Kat."

I lift up and settle on my heels, pulling her hips up to maintain connection, all so I can slide one hand between us. Zeroing in on her clit, I repeat my actions earlier, pinching and rolling it. Within seconds, Kat's back is arched and she's screaming my name, her pussy clenching down on my cock so damn hard. I hurtle into my own orgasm right after her, burying myself in her as I come and come, and fucking come some more.

Finally, my body stops shuddering with my release and I slowly lower down beside Kat. I kiss her damp forehead before climbing off the bed to go and deal with the condom. When I get back, I slide onto the bed next to her and gather her into my arms. She snuggles in, her head resting on my shoulder and our legs tangled together. If anything, this feels just as intimate as what we were just doing.

And I fucking love it.

"Wow," Kat says after a minute, her voice rough. "That was just... Wow."

I let out a low chuckle and press a kiss to the top of her head.

"Damn straight it was, Kitty Kat. Maybe I should change your nickname and call you wildcat instead."

She giggles, slapping my chest lightly. "You're ridiculous." Then she lets out a slow, satisfied sigh. "It's never been like that for me before, you know. I mean, that intense and powerful."

"Same."

And I'm pretty damn sure it never will be again. Because this right here, this is nirvana. This is heaven. This is the best I've ever felt in my life.

CHAPTER THIRTEEN

Kat

"I knew it!" Lily crows the second she walks in my front door. She points at me dramatically. "That is the face of a woman who got laid."

"Could you at least close the door before you announce that?" I hiss, ushering her in the house, my gaze darting around outside to make sure no neighbours were witness to her.

"What's the big deal?" she asks, wandering into my kitchen. "You asked him to the gala in public, everyone knows you're going together."

"Right, but no one knows we're dating." I say, sinking down on one of the stools that lines the counter at my kitchen island.

Lily claps her hands together under her chin. "So, you *are* dating."

I lift my shoulders up and let them fall, a small smile forming. "I mean, yeah? We've gone out for dinner, and then we went snowshoeing yesterday."

"And the sex. Don't forget the sex."

I blush. "Yeah. The sex."

"I want to hear all about it." Lily turns toward me, two cups of coffee in hand. She's well acquainted with my kitchen and knows just how to make coffee for us both. Memories of the morning after Hunter slept on my couch come back, and his reaction to trying my peppermint mocha creamer. He was so cute.

I desperately wanted a repeat of that morning today, but Hunter insisted on going home last night. Even after making me see stars no less than three times, he wouldn't stay over. It made no sense to me, his reaction to the very idea of being seen leaving my house when it wasn't an issue the night his furnace broke down, but I was too scared to push him to explain. We're too new, too fresh, for me to rock the boat.

"Okay, I can tell by the dreamy look on your face you're thinking of him."

Taking a sip of my coffee, I look at Lily. I could use some encouragement and advice, and she's the only one who knows what's going on. "That's the problem, Lil. I can't stop thinking about him. He's so sweet, and charming, and funny, and —"

"You had better be about to tell me he's good in bed. Please tell me he's good in bed," Lily interrupts me.

I just smirk over the top of my coffee cup. "He's good. He's really good."

Lily shrieks, her hand slapping mine. "Yes, girl!"

After our giggles subside, I keep going. "But he doesn't want anyone to know we're together."

Lily frowns. "Why not? He does realize you're freaking amazing, right? He doesn't seem like the kind of guy to have sordid affairs."

"Who the heck says 'sordid affairs' anymore?" I ask, then

shake my head. "Never mind. No, it's not that. He's just worried about what my brothers would say, and he wants to talk to Leo first. He is his boss, after all."

"And he's your cousin. So what?"

She makes a good point, and I don't have an answer. Keeping my eyes on the coffee cup in front of me, I give a small shrug. "I don't know. But something is holding him back, Lily."

"You really like him."

Looking up, I simply nod, feeling the truth of her statement in my soul. "I really do. So, I guess if he needs things to be a secret for now, then I have to respect that."

Lily tilts her head to the side, studying me for a minute, before she nods, too. "Okay. As long as you're happy, I'm happy. A secret sordid affair it is."

Despite my earlier conversation with Lily, never in a million years did I picture myself with a secret boyfriend. Sure, in high school, when my brothers threatened to throat-punch any guy who did me wrong, I debated keeping my relationships secret, but I never actually did.

Not that I dated much, but I had one boyfriend senior year and went on a couple of dates before that. And not once did we worry about people seeing us together.

Yet, here I am, sneaking out the back door of my house in the early evening darkness after leaving lights on at my place so it looks like I'm home, and crossing into my next-door neighbour's yard where he's waiting at *his* back door.

The kiss he gives me in greeting almost makes up for the madness of it all.

"Mmm, if we don't stop now, I'll burn dinner," Hunter mumbles against my mouth, taking an exaggerated step back. "You're addicting, Kat Donnelly."

I trail after him into his kitchen where an incredible aroma awaits. Hunter passes me a glass of wine before picking up his own and going to the stove to stir something.

"Wait a minute, are you telling me not only are you hot, sweet, funny, and good in bed, but you cook as well? Be still my beating heart," I say, pretending to swoon into a chair.

Hunter shoots me a grin over his shoulder. "I'll be honest, there's only a few things in life I would say I'm really good at, but cooking is one of them." He lifts a pan off the stove and dishes something onto two plates. He sprinkles something on top, then carries them over to the table and sets them down with a flourish. "Seafood and vegetable paella. Voilà."

I close my eyes, letting out a small moan as the scent of seafood, tomatoes, and spices hits me. "Oh my God, this smells incredible." When my eyes flutter open, he's staring at me with such intensity, I gasp.

"Dinner first. Then I'm going to feast on you for dessert, Kitty Kat," he growls, and I gasp again, this time louder. He leans over me, crowding me on the chair, but I don't feel closed in; I feel surrounded, protected, and adored. "I honestly don't know how I stayed away for so long once you were single. Everything about you is perfect and so damn irresistible." His lips find mine, and the kiss is surprisingly soft and sweet, at odds with the intensity of his position and energy.

I thread my arms around his neck and pull him closer, deepening the kiss. "Good thing we came to our senses, huh?"

His tongue plunges into my mouth, tangling with mine as our kiss grows sloppy, desperate, needy.

I could kiss this man for hours and never tire of the feel of him, the taste. The sounds he makes, they're so full of satisfaction — and anticipation — it's the ultimate feminine power trip knowing I can affect him so strongly.

Somehow, and I don't know if I'm disappointed or impressed, Hunter finds the restraint and control he needs to pull back, putting some space between us. But just when I think he's going to follow through with the meal, he surprises me.

"Damn it. Fuck dinner."

I get no other warning before Hunter's hands are on my waist, and he's lifting me out of the chair and spinning me around before setting me down on the counter. His eyes are burning with need as he tugs at the hem of my pants.

"Lift."

I scoot forward and lift my butt up just long enough for him to pull my pants and underwear down. Then he drops into a crouch, his hands going to my inner thighs and pushing my legs apart. I'm being manhandled, and I am definitely okay with it. I've never been with a guy like Hunter, who seems to instinctually know what I want and need, and whose wants and needs match mine so perfectly.

He breathes in deeply, his thumbs sliding up my inner thighs, closer and closer to my core. "You're glistening. Such a pretty pussy, so ready for me."

"God, yes," I whisper. "So ready. Please."

His eyes twinkle as he grins. "I've got you, Kitty Kat."

"I need you to…" I start to say, my voice coming out a whine that turns into another gasp as he presses his thumb right onto my clit. "Oh my God. That."

My head falls back against the cabinets with a thunk as he finally leans down and I feel the warmth of his mouth cover my sex. His tongue swirls around, dipping in and out, as his thumb lazily circles my clit, tightening it into a stiff nub.

The kitchen is silent except for the sounds of him eating me out, feasting as he said he would, and my moans and gasps of appreciation.

When he invited me over for dinner, I hoped we'd end up in bed; I'm insatiable for him. But I never expected to be the first course.

Moments later, my orgasm is rocketing through my body as Hunter pins me down to the counter, sucking every drop out of me. His groans and growls reverberate through my body, extending my release until I finally sag against the cabinets, completely spent.

I open my eyes to see him rise to standing, and I drop my gaze down to the obvious bulge in his pants. Licking my lips, I slowly slide off the counter, my pants still down around my ankles. I reach for him, but he steps back.

"No. Dinner."

I arch my brow. "Really?"

Hunter nods, then walks stiffly over to the table, sitting down gingerly before gesturing to my chair. "Yep. I didn't slave over this meal for it to go to waste because I can't keep my hands or mouth off you." He winks, and I slowly make my way to my seat. "You just ended up an appetizer instead of dessert." He cocks his head to one side, as if he's thinking deeply. "Or maybe your pussy can be both. Yeah, I think that works. Sweet and salty, and fucking delicious."

My jaw drops at the filthy words coming out of his mouth, as Hunter casually picks up his wine and takes a sip, his eyes twinkling at me over the glass.

"Eat up, Kitty Kat." His voice takes on a gravelly edge.

Still in a daze, I pick up my fork and take a bite. Even though the food has cooled, the flavours still explode on my tongue. "This is delicious. Who taught you to cook?"

I see him hesitate for the briefest of moments before answering.

"Actually, it was a high school home economics class. At least that's what they called it back then. Our teacher was this amazing woman who sat us all down on day one and told us she didn't care what we thought about domestic duties, everyone — boys and girls alike — needed to know how to sew on a button and prepare a complete meal. And if she caught anyone saying anything different, they'd be on dish duty for the whole term." He chuckles at the memory, smiling fondly. "We started with the basics, and I fell in love with cooking. It was easy to experiment, and pretty soon I was making dinner at home several nights a week. My mom was thrilled, and she and I decided that once a month we would make something totally unique and different. This paella was one of our earlier creations, and I've perfected it over the years."

"Wow. That's an amazing story," I say quietly after he finishes talking. I feel like I've been given the smallest of windows into

Hunter's past, and it makes me realize just how little I know about his life before he moved to Dogwood Cove. He knows so much more about me, simply because of who my family is around here. But he's a mystery. One I desperately want to solve.

"Are you still close to your parents?" I ask, taking another bite of paella.

Hunter gets what I can only describe as a wistful smile on his face. "Yeah. We talk quite a bit, but they had me a lot later in life, so they're getting older and it's hard for them to travel. They still haven't been to Dogwood Cove."

"Where do they live?"

"The house I grew up in, in southern Alberta. I was hoping to visit them over Christmas, but I couldn't get enough days off to make the trip worthwhile. Hopefully, I can go home in the new year."

"They must be so proud of you." I give him a warm smile, but shadows cross his face. "Hunter? Did I say something wrong?"

His stare bores holes into the table in front of him for a moment or two before he lifts his eyes to meet mine. There's a distance there that wasn't present before and it confuses me, as does the half smile he gives me. I'm guessing he means it to be reassuring. It's anything but.

"No. Everything's fine. Would you like more wine?"

The abrupt change in subject has my head spinning a bit, but I can take a hint. I want so badly for him to let me in, tell me what just happened in his mind, but it's so early in our relationship, I don't know if I have the right to push. Every now and then I see these flashes of vulnerability in him. Most of the time, they're so well hidden, no one would know he's anything but the happy-go-lucky, friendly guy he appears to be. But there's something underneath that makes me think it's all a façade.

I just hope that someday he trusts me enough to let me in; let me see all of him. The good and the bad.

Chapter Fourteen

Hunter

After Kat went home last night, I cleaned up the kitchen with what I can only describe as an anxiety-fueled manic state. The energy inside of me was frantic, all-consuming, and chaotic, and I had to get it out.

I want so badly to tell her everything. To tell her how I struggle every fucking day to feel worthy to just breathe the same air as her. But I'm terrified that when she learns what a mess I am, she'll run in the opposite direction. My only strategy right now is to keep my darkness hidden until we're close enough that I can somehow trust her feelings for me, and trust that maybe she'll be able to look past my damage.

Right now, even thinking about it, about letting her in and risking losing her forever, makes me nauseous.

The sex is spectacular. No doubt about that. She's the sweetest, kindest, sexiest woman I've ever met. I desperately want to be able to take her out in public, let everyone know she's my girlfriend, and not hide a thing from anyone.

At least, I want that until the voices creep in, like they did late last night, keeping me up, tossing and turning on sheets that still smelled like her.

Like us.

My shift today doesn't start until the evening, so after dragging my tired ass to the gym, which was thankfully empty, I come home for a long shower, and then I sit on my couch to call my parents.

Because talking about them with Kat last night made me not only miss them, but also realize it's been too long since I had the time for a good conversation with them. And while they might not know everything about my mental health, they know enough to be a safe place for me.

The video chat connects, and I'm staring at the ceiling. "Hey Mom, tilt the phone down so I can see you," I remind her patiently, the way I do every time we talk. She's never really got the hang of technology and figuring out where the camera is on her phone.

"Oh right." There's a rustle, but a few seconds later, I see her face smiling back at me. "Hi honey, how are you, my baby?"

I'm a single child, not because they didn't want more kids but because fertility issues made it impossible. I'm their rainbow baby, coming after too many losses to mention. Which means my parents dote on me, and my mom still calls me her baby. There was a time when it bothered me, but not anymore. Now I know it's simply important for her to show her love any way she can.

"I'm okay. How are you and Dad? Did you get that company to come and plow the driveway again?"

Winter worries me when it comes to my elderly parents. They can't keep up with the snow removal necessary for where they

live, and it's the one regret I have about moving so far away —
not being around to help them. But leaving the small town I
grew up in became absolutely necessary after high school.

It's still hard for me to go back there for any length of time.

Mom and I catch up for a few minutes before she asks the
question I was really hoping she had forgotten to ask.

"And how about that interview for the promotion in the
department? Am I talking to the future Detective Callaghan?"
she asks eagerly, her face beaming with pride.

I hate myself in this moment. Because my only two options
are to disappoint her or lie to her.

"They had to postpone interviews. Maybe in the new year."
The lie falls off my tongue far too easily, but the guilt that comes
with it sits like a stone in my gut. The truth is, I didn't apply.
I didn't think I deserved to. Last I heard, they filled one of the
positions.

But my mom still thinks I'm perfect and amazing, and I don't
have the heart to tell her she's wrong.

"Oh, that's too bad. But I suppose it gives us something to
celebrate when you come home to visit." There's a hopeful
tone, and I don't have the heart to let her down by reminding
her I haven't booked my ticket home yet.

"Yeah. Exactly."

We talk a few minutes more before getting off the phone. As
soon as we do, I go into my bedroom and pull my sweaty gym
clothes back on.

Maybe I can outrun my guilt and self-loathing.

Hasn't worked in the past, but it feels like my only option
right now. Because there's no way I can sit here with these emo-

tions roiling around inside of me like a category three storm.

Despite my mental state, I can't help but feel slightly better when I get to work, and the shift leader communicates what he needs me to do before I go out on patrol. Someone needs to drop off a huge pile of donations we've been collecting all month to the animal shelter, and somehow, I get lucky enough to be assigned the task.

The sky is already darkening by the time I pull into the parking lot, even though it's still early in the evening. I flip up the collar of my uniform jacket as I open the back of the undercover truck I used to haul everything here. Grabbing two large bags of dog food, I toss them over my shoulder. On my way to the front door, I can hear dogs barking in the building, and it makes me smile.

I love animals. They don't judge you if you're sad or worried or think less of you if you can't read very fast. They provide me with a sense of calm and happiness that can often be difficult for me to find.

Then again, Kat gives me that...

Using my hip, I press the button that will automatically open the double front doors. Warmth hits me, along with the unmistakable smell of cleaner and animals. Lots of animals.

There's no one behind the desk out front, so I put down the bags of food and make two more trips to the truck to bring in everything else. On my third trip back inside, Mila Monroe is standing beside the pile of stuff I've brought in, staring at it. She hears me and looks up, understanding coming into her eyes.

"Oh! That's where this is coming from. I thought Santa came early or something."

"Only if Santa is now the Dogwood Cove Police Department," I joke. "Where do you want all of it?"

Mila places her hands on her hips, eyeing the pile of food and toys. "It's more than I was expecting. Which is awesome, don't get me wrong, but I was just in the middle of organizing our storage with —"

"Mila, don't you dare abandon me with all of this." Kat's voice comes down the hall, and two seconds later, there she is, taking my fucking breath away. Even wearing baggy sweats and a hoodie, she's the most gorgeous woman I've ever seen.

"Hunter! What are you doing here?"

I give her a charming grin and a subtle wink, one that I hope says *I really want to come over there and kiss you.* "Just doing my civic duty and dropping off some donations the department pulled together."

She walks over and stands close enough that I could easily touch her. My fingers itch to do just that, but Mila is already eyeing us both. That woman is too nosy for her own good. As much as I hate doing it, I take a step away and pick up the heaviest bag of food. "Show me where to put it?"

We make quick work of moving everything into the storage room which, as Mila started to tell me, is a bit of a mess. I can tell they were working to reorganize everything when I showed up.

"Want me to stay and help get things straightened out?" I offer, even though I really should be getting back to the station for my next assignment.

"Nah, we got this, right Kat?" Mila waves me off. "But thank you for dropping all of this off. And please, thank everyone else at the station. I'll bring some muffins by tomorrow."

"I'm off at six in the morning, can I swing by and get mine on my way home?" I ask hopefully, not wanting to miss out on an apple nut muffin. Mila gives me the thumbs up and turns back to the shelves, only to whirl back around a second later.

"Wait. Hunter. We need your opinion on something."

"Oh my God, no Mila, we don't," Kat interjects, shaking her head wildly. "It was just a crazy idea."

"A crazy *good* idea. And I told you, if you don't want a calendar with your hunky brothers in it, don't buy one."

My eyebrows raise in confusion. "A calendar?"

Mila grins. "Yep. Hunks and Hounds. Kat had the idea to make one as a fundraiser next year." She shakes her head regretfully while Kat, standing off to the side, looks at me with a wild look to her eyes. "Wish we had thought of it sooner, so we had it ready to sell now. What an awesome Christmas gift that would be." She giggles.

"This was your idea?" I ask Kat, fighting back the smirk that wants to break free. "A calendar full of photos of guys and dogs?"

"Not just any guys. Hot guys. Hunks." Mila says.

"You know," I say, that smirk sneaking across my face, "you could take it even further. Hunky *heroes* and hounds. Focus on all the local heroes and first responders."

"That's what I said!" Mila exclaims, then jerks her thumb at Kat. "But this one said it would be gross having a calendar with her brothers in it. I said it's her fault for having a hot family. You know, Hunter, you're pretty hunky. You'd have to be in it, too."

I grin at Mila. "Thanks. I am pretty hunky, and I'm a hero. Win-win. Maybe Kat could just keep her calendar to my photo all year." I'm pushing it, and judging by how her eyes widen, Kat notices. Thankfully, Mila just assumes I'm being me, especially when I wink at her.

"Ha, that's a brilliant idea. See, Kat? Hunter solved your issue."

Kat mumbles something under her breath that I can't understand, but judging by Mila's broad grin, it was a pointed comment directed at her.

This is fun. Being able to flirt with her, all under the guise of simple teasing. Sure, Mila might get suspicious, so I know I have to be careful not to go too far, but then again, I know I've got a reputation of being a charmer, a goofy jokester, and hopefully, that's what she thinks this is.

"Anyway ladies, I had better get going and leave you to your organizing and scheming." I say, and the regret in my voice is only slightly exaggerated. I would much rather hang out here, but I do need to get back to work.

"I'll walk you out so I can lock the front door. We're closed, anyway." Kat walks past me, and after saying goodbye to Mila, I trail after her.

She steps outside with me and immediately starts to shiver. I pull her in close, finally relishing having her in my arms.

"You shouldn't be out here," I mumble into the top of her head.

"I know, I just wanted a hug," she says, her words muffled by my jacket.

I squeeze her even tighter at that. Because damn it, I wanted one, too. Then, reluctantly, I let go.

"Get back inside, Kitty Kat. And text me when you get home later so I know you're okay." I lean down and steal a quick kiss. At least it was meant to be a quick kiss, but just as it always does, it turns into something more within an instant.

When I finally get the strength to pull back, there's a soft, dreamy expression on her face. And I can't help but internally puff up with some pride that I put it there.

"Inside, babe. Now. I don't need a Kat popsicle."

"Okay, okay. I'm going." She turns and puts her hand on the door before looking back over her shoulder. "Hey, Hunter."

"Yeah?"

"I'm glad I got to see you today." Her smile fills me with warmth.

"Me too, Kitty Kat. Me too."

CHAPTER FIFTEEN

Kat

"All I'm saying is, *Die Hard* is the best Christmas movie."

"And all I'm saying is, *The Grinch* is the best Christmas movie. But only the original version with Boris Karloff."

Hunter squeezes my hand, and I lean my head down against his shoulder. My stomach hurts a little from laughing so hard, but that's the way it is with him. He has this capacity to make everything so much fun. Like tonight, all we did was go to a movie. But the entire time, sitting in the back row, Hunter was whispering his running commentary to me, making it almost impossible for me to hold back my giggles. I'm surprised we didn't get kicked out, honestly, for making too much noise.

When we leave the theater, the debate about the best Christmas movie starts up. And when Hunter takes my hand, threading his fingers in mine, I mentally kick my heels in excitement. He's normally so careful — too careful if you ask me — about public displays of affection in case someone we know is around.

But then, to my dismay, we reach the small café where Hunter insisted we stop for some dessert, and he drops my hand to open the door for me.

"What was it you said I needed to try?" I ask, hanging my coat on the back of my chair. "Pecan something?"

Hunter rolls his eyes and gives an exaggerated moan. "Oh, heck yeah. The maple bourbon pecan pie. Best. Dessert. Ever."

I sit down and lean forward, dropping my voice to a whisper. "I thought you said I was the best dessert ever."

His eyes grow dark with lust as he leans over the table, bringing our faces close together. "Good point. Pie is officially the second best."

"Kat?"

I jerk back at the sound of a familiar voice, and Hunter does the same. I look up at Kelly, the manager of The Nutty Muffin, who's approaching our table with her boyfriend Jensen. She looks between the two of us quizzically, and I brace myself for them to ask what the heck is going on. But they don't.

"Hey, Kelly," I say, the words sounding shrill to my ears. "What are you doing here?"

She tilts her head at me but smiles. "We live a few streets over. Everyone knows the maple bourbon pecan pie is the best around, and I was craving a slice."

"It *is* good pie." Hunter chimes in. He turns on his mega-watt grin, the one I am now almost certain is a front for when he's worried or nervous about something.

Kelly nods enthusiastically, tugging on Jensen's hand. I don't know him well, but from what Mila says, they were friends for a long time before finally admitting their feelings for each other.

Kind of like Hunter and me, I guess.

"See? Told you it was good. It's not just me," Kelly says excitedly. "Anyway, we'll leave you two alone, we've got a hot date with our couch, some pie, and some Christmas movies."

"*Die Hard*?" Hunter asks, and Jensen chuckles.

"You know it."

We say our goodbyes, and Kelly and Jensen leave. Turning back to Hunter, I take in the tight lines of his body, full of tension. I'm guessing he was worried they'd ask why we were out together.

"Well, at least it was just Kelly and Jensen, and not The Walkie Talkies that saw us." I try to make a joke because Hunter is obviously withdrawing. And the crack in my confidence that follows is really uncomfortable. "Hunter —" I start to reach my hand over to him, but he pulls it back at the last minute. "We need to tell everyone about us," I say quietly, looking down at the hot chocolate in front of me. "I hate having to hide."

I hear his sigh, and it makes me lift my head.

"I know. I hate it, too."

"So, when should we tell my family? That's the first step, isn't it?"

He's tearing the paper napkin in front of him into tiny pieces, his brow furrowed. I ache to reach over and smooth it out, but even that won't take away whatever is holding him back. I have my suspicions about what's going on in his head, but I don't want to say anything. He needs to come to me, and I can only hope he does when he's ready.

"How about the gala?" I ask. "Everyone will be there, so we get it over with all at once."

The waitress chooses that second to set down plates with our slices of pie in front of us. After she leaves, I don't lift my fork, even though the dessert smells incredible.

Finally, Hunter looks up at me. "Okay. Yeah, let's tell them at the gala." He purses his lips, then slowly relaxes them into a small smile. "Can we eat some pie now?"

I make myself smile back at him, and finally pick up a forkful of pie and bring it to my mouth. "Holy crap, that's delicious."

Now his smile grows. "Told you."

Hunter pulls into his driveway and cuts the engine. The silence is deafening for a split second. Then his lips are on the patch of bare skin at the base of my neck.

"Can I come over?" he asks, and the hesitation in his voice makes my heart ache.

"Of course."

We get out, and I pretend not to notice Hunter checking the street to make sure none of our neighbours are out.

I'm starting to really hate this. The novelty of dating in secret is wearing off fast. And in its place is my own worry that maybe I won't like the reason for the secrecy. That maybe it'll be something we can't overcome.

Once we're inside, we make our way down the hall to my bedroom, both of us lost in our heads.

I undress to my bra and panties and slide into bed facing him. Hunter, clad only in his boxer briefs, does the same, and we lay there, mirror images of each other in the dark silence.

"Hunter."

"Kat."

The tension breaks as we speak simultaneously, and we both

let out a low chuckle. Hunter's arm snakes out and wraps around my hip, pulling me into his arms. I snuggle in, my head resting on his chest.

"Will you stay tonight?" I ask quietly, already knowing the answer.

"I can't risk someone seeing me in the morning."

"You could go through the back door."

"I didn't leave mine unlocked and I don't have the right keys."

A small disappointed sigh escapes me, and Hunter rolls me onto my back, moving over me. "I'm sorry, Kitty Kat. But we'll tell everyone soon, and then we won't have to sneak around. Please, please be patient with me."

His lips find mine and he kisses me, desperation mixing with need. I kiss him back, trying to lose myself in his touch. His hands slide under my back, he unhooks my bra, and I shrug it off. His mouth trails down my body until he covers my breast with his kiss.

"I need you, Kat. Just be patient. Please." He lifts his head up to look at me, and the wild look in his eyes scorches me to my heart.

"I will be. I need you, too," I whisper. He surges up to kiss my lips again, his hands touching me everywhere, lighting me up. My legs fall open, and I start to rock underneath him, the friction from my panties amplifying the sensation of his length sliding up and down on me.

"Now, please, Hunter," I gasp.

He tears off his underwear, then mine. Grabbing a condom from my bedside drawer, I watch him roll it on with shaky hands and then he's back, covering me and thrusting inside in one motion.

We start to make love, and it's raw, messy, and fast. There's no romance, but it's no less intimate. I can feel something coiling around us, dark and worrisome. But I push it back. He's here with me, and that's all that matters. We can figure everything else out later.

"Kat, I'm sorry, babe. It's fast. I can't —" Hunter starts babbling, his movements frantic and chaotic to match his wild eyes. His hands are gripping the sheets beside me.

I wrap my arms tighter around his shoulders and do my best to match his thrusts. This isn't for me right now. This is for him. "It's okay, Hunter. I'm here. Let go."

He cries out my name, his face dropping into the crook of my neck as I feel his release. Eventually, he stops moving, and his body sags down on top of me. I relish the feel of his heavy weight on me and move to turn my head so I can kiss him. But he doesn't look my way. Instead, he rolls off and away from me, leaving a chill in his place.

I start to speak, to ask him if he's okay, but he bolts out of the room, and the next thing I hear is the bathroom door shutting firmly.

Shutting me out.

My heart squeezes painfully in my chest. *What. The. Heck. Was. That.*

CHAPTER SIXTEEN

Hunter

I put trembling hands on Kat's bathroom counter and let my head hang down. What the fuck is wrong with me? I don't know what that was out there, me running away leaving her unsatisfied and probably confused as fuck, but it wasn't anything she deserves.

I should just leave. Make up an excuse and leave.

But I can't do that to her. Somehow, she's become the most important thing in my life. She is the only thing that comes even remotely close to having the power to snap me out of the kind of mental slump that has creeped up on me tonight. Which is at odds with the fact that my relationship with her has *caused the slump.*

Pushing off the counter, I stare at myself in the mirror. Kat Donnelly has chosen me as the man she wants to be with. No goddamn way am I going to take that for granted. Not for a second.

"Man up, Callaghan," I whisper to my reflection. It's never that easy, I know. If I could erase my anxiety with just a few words of self talk, I'd be fine. But that does nothing to tame the beast.

However, at least for now, the bigger beast is the mess I just made with Kat, and *that* gives me enough courage to face her.

When I go back into the bedroom, she's sitting up, leaning against the headboard with her knees drawn up and the sheet covering most of her body. She's fidgeting with her fingers, and my heart sinks. I hate that I made her feel like anything less than the amazing woman she is.

"Kat, I'm sorry. That was..." I trail off, running my hands through my hair. "I don't know how to explain what that was, but it wasn't okay."

I approach slowly, relief flooding me when she looks up and pats the bed beside her. At least she isn't kicking me out. I slide under the sheet and open my arms. Thank fuck, she accepts the invitation and snuggles up against me, her hand coming to rest on my abdomen.

I'm still ready for her to be mad, or at least annoyed, that I ran right after sex. Mediocre sex, at that. But I should have known Kat wouldn't see it that way.

"Don't beat yourself up. Please. Yes, we need to talk about what just happened, but it's okay that you needed something I could give you."

"But you got nothing in return," I say. "Shit, you didn't even come. Fuck, I'm a selfish asshole." I move to roll her under me, determined to rectify things when she stops me, throwing her leg over mine and straddling my waist.

"Hunter. Stop." Her hands come to my chest, and she looks like a beautiful warrior, ready to avenge, well, anything. "I'm not worried about the fact that you got off and I didn't. If anything,

I like that I can do that for you. Make you let go completely."

Her body sags slightly when she stops talking, her hands resting on my chest. The strength and conviction fades and are replaced by something that makes my stomach turn over. I watch as she bites her lower lip, her eyes downcast, and wait to see if she'll call me out on my bullshit. But she doesn't, which means it's on me.

"What aren't you saying?" I ask quietly, tilting her chin back up so she's looking at me. "What do you need, Kitty Kat? What can I do?"

"You can let me in," she whispers. "I know there's more going on inside your heart and your head than what you tell me. Let me in, Hunter."

I hear the pleading tone of her voice. She's right, she gave me what I needed — the opportunity to just let go and lose myself in her, but I can't give her what she needs. God, I want to. So fucking badly. But I can't, not yet.

I don't answer her with words. Instead, I pull her down so I can kiss her, deeply, passionately, intimately. I can't give her the explanation she wants, so I can only hope and pray that giving her a physical connection is enough for now.

Thank God, she relaxes into me automatically. I should feel guilty for avoiding her legitimate and valid request, but I only feel grateful.

Her naked body starts to heat up against mine as my hands travel up and down her spine, one tangling in her hair and the other cupping her ass. She starts to rock her hips, moving up and down my already hardening dick lying between us. My hand slides between her legs, finding the short damp curls that cover her pussy. She lifts her ass slightly, giving me access, her lips leaving mine as she lets out a small gasp.

"Let me make you feel good, babe."

She nods, widening her legs just enough that I can dip two fingers in and out of her, teasing her until she's writhing around on top of me. I bring her close to the edge with just my hand, and when I feel her start to tighten, I lift my upper body, taking her with me so that we're both sitting, facing each other. Reaching over to the bedside table, I grab a condom and somehow manage to roll it on while she's peppering kisses all over my face. Then I grab her hips, lifting slightly so I can line myself up, and then lower her onto my cock.

This time it has to be about her. I rock my hips back and forth in short, shallow movements. Kat's hands come to the back of my head, and then she's gripping my hair, pulling it slightly. I relish the pain, knowing that it means pleasure for her.

"Come for me, Kat," I rumble into her neck, my lips sucking gently, not enough to leave a mark but enough to let her know the intensity of my feelings matches hers.

She lifts her hips up and down, my body meeting her every move. And it's not long before I feel the telltale clench of her body around me. And even though I didn't think I could be ready for another orgasm so soon, especially not with where my head was just moments ago, my own body responds, and then I'm moaning out her name as she chants out mine.

This time, I don't make a run for it. I let her sink into my arms and hold her tightly against me. We're sticky with sweat, but I don't care. Because I can feel her heart racing, and her fingers slowly trailing up and down my spine, and the perfect contradiction of those two things — one fast and intense, one slow and satisfied, is what I need to feel right now.

I kiss her nose, then shift her off me. This time when I slide out of bed, I just tie off the condom, drop it in the garbage can, then go straight back to her side. I'll have to go home soon, but I need a few more minutes with her in my arms.

"Are you okay now?" she asks once we're tangled up again.

I nod, kissing the top of her head. But it's a lie.

I should feel better now that I've made her come, now that I've brought her pleasure and put a satisfied, dreamy smile on her face. But I don't.

Because it's not enough. I'll never be able to give her enough.

The following afternoon, Steve Larabee drags me out of the station for lunch. The man is remarkably stubborn and when I muttered that I was good with something from the vending machine, he just shook his head and told me I had five seconds to get up and grab my jacket or he'd convince Leo to put me on traffic duty for a month.

I don't know how he figures he'd do that, but it's not a risk I'm willing to take, so I join him. Of course, the very reason I don't want to go to Camille's today is the first thing I see when we walk in.

She's like a magnet for my eyes; I find her in an instant. And her beauty just about brings me to my knees. Her hair is braided down her back, and she's wearing jeans and a soft sweater. But it's the smile on her face as she talks to Pete and

Turner, two older men who live in town and come in for lunch every Tuesday. She told me once that they've ordered the exact same thing every week, ever since Mila opened the café a couple years ago.

You gotta admire commitment like that.

Steve and I sit down at the long counter and place our orders with the guy working the cash register. It takes physical effort for me not to seek out Kat. When I left last night, she seemed okay. Disappointed I wouldn't stay but accepting just the same. But her disappointment stayed with me, kept me up all night, and is the reason why I didn't want to come here today.

Not that I didn't want to see her, but I didn't want to have to disappoint her again. Which feels inevitable when I'm the reason we're still keeping this all under wraps.

"Hello gentlemen," her soft voice washes over me, and I long to reach out and pull her into my arms.

"Hey Kitty Kat," I say, injecting a casual tone into my voice. "How's it going?"

"Fine, thank you." She gives me a smile that is so full of heat and promise, my eyes dart over to Steve to make sure he doesn't see it. I don't know what I expected from her today, but it wasn't this. I figured she'd still be at least a little bummed about last night. But maybe I'm the only one overthinking and worrying about every goddamn thing.

Part of me is jealous of her ability to move on so easily, the other part of me is incredibly grateful she doesn't have to live with the dark cloud over her head that I have.

"Good. That's good." I give her a smile back. If we're playing it casual, I better keep up appearances. "Are you ready for the gala this weekend?"

A faint blush covers her cheeks as she tugs her lower lip in between her teeth. "Yep. I'm looking forward to it." Her eyes fill with something that a distant part of my heart wants to say might be love, but there's no way.

No. Way.

"You guys are going together, right?" Steve interrupts. Fuck, I'd forgotten he was even there.

"Yeah, Hunter agreed to keep me company," Kat answers casually.

Those words sit in my stomach like a lead weight. Keep her company? Is that what she's telling people? I feel awful for never stopping to really think how she might be handling this. I'm betting Steve isn't the first person to ask who she's going with or make a comment about the two of us going together. And I just left her out hanging in the wind, unable to say anything about why we're going together or what it means.

Fuck.

"It'll be nice to spend time with my family, too." She looks at me pointedly, and I have to force a smile to my face, hoping it doesn't turn out a grimace instead. I didn't need the reminder that I promised to come clean to her family at the gala. The less I think about it, the better. Her face falls when I say nothing. It's slight, but I see it. I see everything when it comes to Kat.

"Well, you enjoy your lunches. I better get back to work." Kat starts to walk away, then pauses and turns back. "Oh, Hunter, I was going to ask, could you pop over after work and take a look at something for me in my kitchen? I'd ask my brothers but they're all busy."

"Sure, of course." I nod, and I can't help the fact that my eyes follow her as she walks away.

"Are you really just keeping her company at the gala or is there something more going on?"

I jerk around and stare at Steve. "What?"

He shrugs and picks up the sandwich that was just set down in front of him by another waitress. "Just sayin', if it were me that Kat Donnelly was the least bit interested in, I'd be locking that down fast."

I say nothing. Because anything I would say feels like it would only dig the hole I'm in even deeper. After all, he's not wrong. If I were a smarter, braver, *better* man, I would have made it clear to everyone that Kat's mine right from the start.

I have to do better. She deserves better.

I just don't know how to convince myself I'm capable of that.

Chapter Seventeen

Kat

"Girl, when Hunter sees you in that dress…" Lily makes a chef's kiss motion with her hands. "He is going to just die."

I twist back and forth, looking down my body, trying to check all angles for any embarrassing lines. Thankfully, the lace thong I'm wearing is smooth against my skin, and the fabric of the dress hangs perfectly.

"You think so?" I smooth my hands down the front of my deep maroon coloured sheath dress. It does fit me really, *really* well, and the jewel tone of the fabric sets off my hair nicely. I've had this dress sitting in my closet for almost a year, just waiting for the right time to wear it.

And a fancy party when I'll finally get to let the world know Hunter and I are together seems like the perfect time.

"You look like a Christmas present ready for him to unwrap." Lily shakes her head slowly. "I'm going to get out of here so you and your man can have a moment alone when he picks you up. But…" Lily draws out that one word with a smirk. "If you aren't at the gala in less than one hour from now, I'm telling your brothers about the two of you dating."

"Don't you dare, or I'll tell everyone about the time you were laughing so hard at Mexican night you snorted queso out your nose."

Lily shoots daggers at me. "Fine. But I'm tired of keeping this secret."

"You and me both," I reply drily.

Her face shifts into a sympathetic smile. "Tonight's the night. Just don't let Hunter keep you too long. And if he messes up your makeup, I'll be able to tell. Bye, babe."

After she leaves, I walk downstairs and stand in front of my mirror for several more minutes. The memories of Hunter standing almost where I am now and telling me to watch while he made me shatter with pleasure have been on repeat ever since our first night together.

Every time we've made love, I have asked him to stay. And every time he's come up with a reason not to. And it all comes back to his need to keep our relationship a secret.

But that ends tonight.

"Thank God we won't have to hide any longer," I whisper to myself just as the doorbell rings. With one last check of my lip stain that claims to be transfer-proof — *guess we'll see about that* — I pick up my clutch and my coat and turn to the door to let him in.

As soon as I open the door, Hunter's mouth falls open. His hand comes up to cover it, rubbing his jaw in appreciation. "Goddamn, Kitty Kat. If you didn't want to go to the fundraiser, you could've just told me so. No need to tempt me like this. I'm a sure thing, babe."

I slap his chest, laughing. "Nice try, buddy. But I'm glad you like the dress."

"The dress, the shoes, everything." Hunter takes my hand and twirls me. "You're gorgeous. Absolutely, breathtakingly gorgeous." He leans in and presses a sweet kiss to my cheek, then trails his lips over to my ear. "And those shoes are gonna be the only thing that stays on when we get home later. Got it?"

My entire body shivers in anticipation. "Got it," I whisper back.

Hunter releases me and helps me into my coat. Once my door is locked, he tucks my arm in his elbow, leading me down the path to his car.

"Being a gentleman again tonight, I see," I tease as he holds the door open for me.

"Only till we're between the sheets, Kitty Kat," he murmurs seductively, giving me a wink as he closes the car door.

I take off my coat once I'm in since the car is plenty warm. When Hunter slides into his seat, his eyes travel up and down my body as he gives his head a slow shake. "Damn. You just... Wow."

His response is exactly what I wanted. And the heat of his hand on my leg, the entire drive to Westport where the gala is being held, is a promise of things to come.

When we get to the hotel where the party is taking place, Hunter pulls into a parking spot and turns the car off but makes no move to get out. Somehow, the energy in the air has changed over the last few minutes from heated and flirtatious to tense and somber.

"Hunter?" I ask, confused and just a little worried.

"I need a second to get ready to face the firing squad," he

mumbles.

I laugh nervously, because that makes it sound like I'm taking him to meet his doom in there, when in reality, it's just our family and friends.

"I won't lie, I'm a little nervous, too," I start to say. "This feels like a big deal, but really, it isn't."

Hunter flashes me an indiscernible look. "Yeah, it is. Are you sure you want to tell everyone tonight that we're dating? There's no rush, is there? Things are good right now."

Something in my gut flip-flops.

"Things are good, but they'll be even better when we don't have to hide. And we planned to do it tonight when everyone's here, to get it over with," I reason. Hunter nods. But something's off. I'm pretty sure I've seen him nervous before, but this is heavier than that, more intense. "Hey, where's the calm, cool, collected cop who saved me from a snowy highway?" I say lightly, twisting in my seat so I can reach my hand over to rest it on his chest. Hunter covers it with his own, squeezing gently.

"Honestly? Work and the gym are pretty much the only two places I can shut this part of my stupid fucking brain off."

My eyebrows draw together in confusion, even as understanding starts to dawn on me. Meanwhile, Hunter looks like he swallowed a lemon, or more likely, didn't mean to admit that.

"What do you mean?" I ask quietly. *Is this the moment he'll finally let me in?*

His head hits the headrest as his eyes stare up at the roof. I can sense the battle in his brain about how to handle his confession, and all I can do is hope he'll be honest.

"I probably should have told you this before things started

between us. So, I understand if you don't want anything to do with me after I tell you this." His eyes close. "I have general-ized anxiety disorder. Diagnosed as a teenager. Makes me worry about stupid shit, overthink everything, and basically feel like I'll never be good enough. Makes me a fucking mess most of the time, and barely functional the rest of the time."

Oh. *Oh.* Suddenly, a lot of things that made me pause over the last few weeks are starting to make sense. His reaction to me at the café the day after our first date. The worry over telling my family we're dating. Heck, maybe even him not going for that promotion Leo was talking about.

His anxiety is the cause of all of it. If I'm honest, I think a part of me knew something like this was going on. But I'd also been worried there was some other worse reason for Hunter being so concerned about people finding out about us.

What that could be, who knows, but I was starting to really freak out that it was something we couldn't figure our way through. Whereas this, this I can handle. I can be beside him and help him. Or at least, I can try. He needs to know I'm not going anywhere just because he has anxiety.

"I think you're good enough," I say quietly. "More than good enough, in fact. You're amazing, Hunter Callaghan. You're hardworking, kind, friendly, good in bed," I add that last one teasingly, and finally, he cracks a smile. "And sexy as hell. I don't care that you have anxiety. I'm grateful you told me, and I want to help. But most importantly, I'm so happy you're here with me tonight."

I get no warning before Hunter's upper body lunges across the car, pinning me against the door, interrupting my thought.

His lips cover mine in a desperate, plundering kiss. I meet him stroke for stroke, trying to infuse it with all the reassurances and support I possibly can.

I'm in danger of falling in love with this man. No, it might be too late for that. I think I *am* falling in love with him. Which I never thought I would feel brave enough to do again after Tyson cheated on me. But Hunter makes me brave. And tonight, after the party is over, and our relationship is out in the open, I'm going to tell him. Maybe then he'll understand exactly what I think of him and how I feel about us.

Eventually, our lips part, both of us breathing heavily. My thumb comes up to trace along his lip. "They really meant it when they said transfer-proof."

Hunter raises his eyebrows. "Say what?"

I giggle, happy to have broken the tension. "My lipstick. The brand promises it's transfer-proof, and since you aren't wearing 'raspberry charm' on your mouth, I'm assuming it worked."

His low laugh fills the car.

"Ready to go in now?"

He nods, climbs out of the car, and walks around to open my door. As soon as I'm out, he pulls me in for a crushing hug. "Thank you for not running in the opposite direction."

I reach up to touch his cheek. "Anyone who runs away from you would have to be an idiot."

"Or a criminal," he quips, and we both laugh. Taking my hand in his, we make our way to the door.

As soon as we're inside, however, any progress we made in the car at taming Hunter's anxiety is lost. His eyes dart everywhere, and his hand starts to squeeze mine uncomfortably tight. I see his chest rising and falling rapidly.

I try to take in the tasteful Christmas décor that fills the ballroom, but the tension coming from Hunter is palpable.

"Do you think your family is here yet? I don't see them. Shit, I really should've talked to Leo before tonight."

"Shoulda, woulda, coulda." I shrug, trying to make light of things. "They're not going to have a problem with us dating, Hunter. I know I made it seem like they scare off every guy I date, but we're two consenting adults. Even my neanderthal brothers will get that."

Hunter won't meet my gaze; he's still scanning for my idiot brothers. "That's not what I'm worried about."

"Then what is it? You can take them," I try teasing him, but even that doesn't seem to get through the haze of worry clouding him.

"You know Sawyer has basically told every single first responder in town to keep their hands off you. He says no one is good enough for you. Pretty sure he didn't mean I would be the exception to that. Especially not if he knew the truth about me."

His disparaging tone is directed at himself, but now my own insecurities are starting to bubble to the surface. Maybe we can't overcome his anxiety if it's this paralyzing for him because I have no clue what to do. All the progress we made in the car is gone.

What if his anxiety isn't about facing my brothers after all? What if the truth is that Hunter doesn't care for me the way I do him and he doesn't want to go public because he doesn't really want to be with me?

"Hunter, do you not want to be here with me right now? Is that it?" I blurt out, unable to hold back my own fears.

"God, no!" he says, his mouth falling open. "Fuck, Kat. No. I'm so sorry. Here you are, the most beautiful woman on earth, and I'm a nervous sack of shit, ruining everything. I want to be with you. I swear I do. I'm just... Fuck." He runs his hand through his hair, and while his response eases my own worries somewhat, it does nothing to stop my pain at hearing him beat himself up so much.

"Why you ever thought I was worthy of being with you, I will never understand. You're a goddess, Kat. A fucking goddess." He looks at me and the emotions swimming in his eyes make my heart hurt for him. What the hell happened in the past to make this beautiful man think so little of himself?

It's a struggle, but I manage to tamp down my own nerves. I have to trust him, trust that he's being honest about wanting to be with me. He trusted me with his confession about the anxiety, so I have to trust him with this. He needs me to be strong for both of us right now, and so that's what I'll do.

Taking in a deep breath, I lift my hand to stroke back the lock of hair that I love so much. "Every goddess needs her god," I murmur, shifting so my body is tucked up against his chest. All I want to do is make him see himself the way I do. As a strong, charismatic, thoughtful, sexy man.

If words don't center him, maybe physical touch will.

Sure enough, his body softens against mine and his hands slide around my hips to meet at the base of my spine. I tangle my hands together behind his neck, relishing the exhale of his stress as his forehead drops to meet mine.

I lower my voice to a sultry whisper, meant for his ears only. "We're in this together, Hunter. You and me. And after the party, we'll go home, and I'll show you exactly why I think you're more than enough."

"Kitty Kat, you're too fucking good to me. But I promise I'm gonna try to stop letting my own shit get in the way and just be —"

"What the actual *fuck* is going on here?"

CHAPTER EIGHTEEN

Hunter

I step back so damn fast, my hands fall away from her body. It's the wrong reaction. I know this the second I see the look of confusion and hurt on Kat's face. I promised her I could do this, and I lied.

"Why the hell are your hands all over my sister, Callaghan?"

Sawyer Donnelly is glaring at me, and if looks could kill, I'd be six feet under already.

"Sawyer, shut up! You're making a scene," Kat hisses. She reaches for my hand, but I shift away, lifting my hands up in a defensive gesture instead.

"Sorry, Sawyer," I mumble. Wrong thing to say yet again, given the glare Kat whips my way. I guess that's fair; he's not the one who deserves an apology. But adrenaline is pumping through my system and my entire body wants to flee.

"He's *my date*, you overbearing asshole," she shoots at her brother.

God, she's on fire. And it's a beautiful thing to witness, Kat in all her glory, standing up for me. So why are all my instincts screaming at me to run?

"He might be your date, but that doesn't give him the right to paw at you," Sawyer fires back, alternating his glare between me and Kat.

Leo and Serena make their way over with Kat's oldest brother Max, and my need to get out of this situation intensifies.

"What's going on, guys?" Serena asks.

"Sawyer's being a goddamn neanderthal, that's what," Kat says, venom dripping from her words. For now, it's directed at her brother. But I deserve it, too.

Or at least I will.

"We're just friends. It's nothing."

The second the lie leaves my mouth, I want to take it back. My heart feels like I just ran it through a fucking meat grinder. She's so much more than that. She's everything.

"What?" Kat whispers, just barely loud enough for everyone to hear. I can't bring myself to look at her. Instead, I keep my eyes locked on Sawyer Donnelly.

"Just friends?" he growls after a minute of staring intensely at me. I nod, my fists clenched at my sides as I will my body to stay where it is and face him.

"Then why is our sister leaving in tears?"

That breaks my focus. My head whips around just in time to see the back of Kat's head, Serena's arm wrapped around her shoulders as they leave the room.

"Fuck." To my surprise, my urge to run is replaced by a stronger one — the urge to follow her and beg for forgiveness. Not that I deserve it.

"Yeah. So, yet again, I'm gonna ask why the hell your hands were all over her, and what did you do to hurt her?" Sawyer steps closer to me, close enough I can see a vein jumping in his neck.

"This isn't the time or place," Leo interjects, sliding between us. "Take a step back, Sawyer, and calm the fuck down."

There's a moment of tense silence, then thank fuck, Sawyer listens to his cousin. He gives me one final glare before pivoting and storming away.

Max looks at me, his eyes troubled. "I don't know you well enough to pass judgment, Hunter, but I don't like seeing my sister upset. So, whatever the fuck just went down, it's not okay."

"Max, can you just go make sure Sawyer doesn't do anything stupid?" Leo asks his cousin calmly. "I need to talk to Hunter."

The oldest Donnelly nods slowly before following his brother. Leo turns to me, but I'm frozen. Locked in place, staring at the door Kat just left through, wondering how the hell I let this go so wrong. Maybe I should let Sawyer beat the shit out of me, like he obviously wants to.

Now that, I deserve.

"Callaghan. What the goddamn hell was that?" Leo starts in a harsh whisper.

"Leo, I..."

"Shut up and listen, Hunter."

My mouth snaps shut.

"I don't buy that 'just friends' shit for a second. And if I'm right, you need to fix this. Because Sawyer and the other boys will calm down. They talk a big talk, but Kat knows how to handle them. Unless you hurt her for real. Then all bets are off, and it won't be only the Donnelly brothers gunning for you."

Leo Talbot is an intimidating man when he wants to be. And

right now, every inch of him is glowering down at me with full force as not only my superior, but a man who cares about the woman whose heart I just destroyed.

"You should go home, Hunter. Think about what happened here tonight, and how the hell you're going to fix things with Kat. Because I don't like seeing my cousin hurting like she is right now."

He's giving me an out and I'm gonna take it before the rest of the Donnelly family finds me. No goddamn way can I face Kat's parents right now. I give Leo a curt nod and hustle my ass out of the hotel.

What have I done?

I don't know how I manage to make it home without crashing my car. Between the tremors in my hands and my racing thoughts, I'm definitely a liability on the road.

Blindly, I push through my front door, not letting myself even chance a glance over to Kat's house. I drop my keys God knows where, loosen my tie, and fling it along with my jacket down on the floor. Going into my kitchen, I grab the bottle of tequila Ash brought back from Mexico last year and drop down on my couch.

But as the first burn of liquor goes down my throat, instead of the oblivion I thought I wanted, I feel only shame and regret. Which is why I make the smartest decision all night and send an email to my therapist requesting an emergency appointment tomorrow.

Then I get drunk.

"Hello, Hunter. It's been a while. I must admit, I was surprised to see your email last night. Can you tell me what it is that caused you to reach out?"

Looking at the compassionate yet detached face of Audrey, my therapist, through the screen of my computer, I finally have the epiphany I needed to have a day ago.

For years, Audrey was my safe person. The one who knows *everything* about me, my anxiety, and my past. She's been the only person I truly felt I could be vulnerable with and not risk judgment.

Yeah, I know, she's a goddamn professional. I literally pay her hundreds of dollars to be that for me.

But looking at her face today, I realize she isn't the only person who makes me feel safe anymore. Kat does, too, and I'm terrified I might have lost her simply by being too damn scared to tell her.

I can only hope I'm not too late.

"Do you remember Becky?" I ask. It's an odd way to start my confession, but Audrey knows when I've escalated my brain works in pretty disjointed ways. She's good at following me.

"I do. That was your high school girlfriend, correct?"

I nod. "Yeah. We dated for two years. Even though we were young, I honestly thought I might marry her one day. She came with me to the hospital when I had my first panic attack, and she's the first person I told when I was finally diagnosed with anxiety and my learning disability."

Audrey writes something down off screen, then turns her eyes back to me. "What makes you bring her up today, Hunter?" She never hesitates to get to the root of things. It's why I still use her as my therapist, years later. She cuts through any bullshit and helps me see things straight. I just hope she can help me see a way through *this*.

"When she broke up with me, she basically said she was better off without me because of my issues. And I took that to heart. I spent the next decade never getting too close to a woman, and never letting anyone outside of my family and closest friends know about my learning disability or my anxiety."

Audrey nods again. "Yes. I recall we spent several months unpacking those feelings and working on strategies to help you remember your value is not dependent on other people's opinions."

"Right. Except I never had the chance to put those strategies to work. I never field-tested them. And when I finally needed them, they failed. I fucked up, Audrey. I lost the one woman who might have been able to understand me, accept me, and love me." My voice cracks.

"Okay. I'm hearing there have been some significant positive changes in your personal life lately, but when you were faced with a challenge in this new relationship, you didn't handle it the way you wish you had. Is that fair?" I nod and Audrey acknowledges me with a tilt of her head. "Alright, when you're ready, why don't you start at the beginning and tell me about this new woman."

I take a deep cleansing breath and send my thoughts back in time to when I first met Kat. The warm summer day I moved in next door and saw her outside wearing cut-off jean shorts and a bikini top as she washed her car, I knew.

I knew something was about to change. I just didn't know

what.

CHAPTER NINETEEN

Kat

I let Serena drive me home from the gala but refused her offer to stay with me a while and talk it out. I wasn't ready for that. The one thing I did ask was that she go back to the party and make sure my parents and Lily knew the basics of what happened and that I needed some time to process things. And most importantly, that they *not* get mad at Hunter. No matter what the boys told them.

Because despite the way my heart is hurting, I still love the man. And when I see headlights flash out front, telling me he's home, probably hurting just as much as I am, my heart breaks even more. I had to stop myself from putting on shoes and going over there to make sure he's okay.

After sitting in a hot bath, letting my tears fall, I go to bed, but there's no chance I'll fall asleep easily. Not with all my emotions racing around in my head.

Somewhere around midnight, I throw back the covers, remembering a mental health course I took last spring. I get up and dig out my notes and texts. Not that learning from a textbook is anywhere near enough, but I need to do something —

anything. And maybe I can gain a bit more understanding of what Hunter lives with every day.

With a cup of chamomile tea, I read through everything, hoping for some glimpse, some nugget that will help me figure out what to do next.

There's no denying I was, and still am, devastated his anxiety got the better of him last night. He tossed aside everything I thought we were building together so easily, ripping my already fragile confidence to shreds in the process. I thought for once I had fallen for a man who felt the same way. Who wanted me as much as I wanted him. I wasn't ignoring the hurdles in front of us, or trying to diminish his fears as not important, but I truly believed he wanted to be with me.

Which is what made the words "just friends" hurt so damn much. No matter how much I try to tell myself it had to be his anxiety talking, it still hurts.

Because why did I try so hard to build him up, to be strong and brave for the both of us, only to have him tear us apart with two stupid words?

Why does this keep happening to me? Why do I keep falling for guys who are unable to give me what I so desperately want — the chance to love someone and be loved in return, openly, wholly, completely.

My eyes are blurry and dry as I roll out of bed after finally managing to get a couple hours of sleep. Somewhere around 3 am, I put down the textbook and climbed back into bed, the tears falling again as I hugged a pillow to my chest, breathing in the faint scent left from the last time Hunter was here with me.

As I stagger into the kitchen in search of coffee, I look around my house. I thought I had cried all of the tears I had inside of me, but a fresh one tracks down my cheek when my eyes catch on the boxes I pulled out of storage yesterday morning.

Hunter and I were meant to be waking up in my bed after a fun night out. I assumed we would finally get to spend an entire night together. We had talked about going out to the Martin family farm to get a tree, and then decorating my house for Christmas.

Instead, I'm alone, and the boxes of decorations in the corner are silent reminders of that. All the understanding and compassion I tried to find between the pages of a book last night doesn't come anywhere close to erasing the sharp pain I felt when he stepped away from me, away from us.

But the longer I stare at those boxes, the more something else starts to creep over me. A sense of determination, but a peaceful determination.

Hunter needs to understand how badly his actions last night hurt me. But he also needs to know he can lean on me, trust me to be there with him when he stumbles. I'm not giving up on Hunter, or on us. I need some time, but I will do everything I can to make him see. Because I truly believe we're better together. And the power of our connection can help him face his fears and worries.

I know it.

The first step is dealing with my brothers. I finish making my coffee and make my way to the couch. Once I'm bundled up under a blanket, I pick up my phone and type out a message that hopefully gets the point across to those boneheads.

KAT: Listen up you jerks. If ANY OF YOU dares interfere or say a damn thing about the man I'm dating ever again, there will be hell to pay. I'm an adult. Fully capable of making my own decisions. So unless there is concern for my immediate safety, back the hell off.

MAX: Are you okay, Kat?

SAWYER: WTF little sis. You can't show up out of the blue with some dude's hands all over your ass and not expect us to react.

BECKETT: Speak for yourself, Sawyer. I think she can. Besides, Hunter isn't just some dude. We know him.

KAT: And that's why Beckett is my favourite brother. Yes Max, I'm fine. Hurt, yes. But not just by what Hunter said. When I'm ready to talk to you idiots again, we'll be having words about this decree Sawyer gave apparently every guy in Dogwood Cove. But for now, if you guys know what's good for you, you'll leave me alone for a few days.

SAWYER: Not every guy. Just the first responders.

MAX: And the entire football team back in high school. Sorry Kat, we'll give you some space. But you know we love you, right?

KAT: I know. But I'm really really mad at you right now. Well, I'm mad at Sawyer. But all of you better back off.

A few seconds later, a reply comes in, not from one of the three brothers who were witness to my heartbreak last night, but from the one who's stuck in another country playing hockey. I can't help the small smile that flashes across my face at Jude's message.

JUDE: What the fucking hell did you asshats do...

Group texts are a wonderful thing, and the ability to *mute* group text conversations is even better. I drop my phone back down on the couch beside me and snuggle under my blanket, turning on the TV. A cheesy holiday movie might be a weird choice given the heartache I'm dealing with, but at the same time, maybe a love story will give me some ideas on how Hunter and I can fix things.

That hope is dashed an hour later as I watch the heroine stand on the sidewalk as her love interest walks away from her. Even though I know how the movie will end, with everyone living happily ever after, my eyes start to fill. "Love sucks," I murmur, dashing away the tears. It's a bit ridiculous to be talking to a TV screen, but I can't help it. The parallel between the story playing out on screen and what happened to me is uncanny.

A knock on my door is followed by the sound of a key in the lock. My gut reaction is to wish it were Hunter, but I know it's not. It's either my mom or Lily, and my money is on the latter, since she doesn't understand the concept of space.

"Kat? Babe? I have alcohol and chocolate. Which do you need?"

"You didn't get the message I needed some time?" I reply, sitting upright and wiping my sleeve across my face as my best friend storms into the living room.

"Nope." She drops down onto the couch next to me and drags me into an awkward hug. "My best friend is hurting. You really think I could stay away?"

I adjust my body slightly and let her squeeze me tightly. "I'm alright, Lil. Really."

She pushes me back and examines me critically. "Hmm. I don't see how that's possible but seeing as there's no empty bottles of wine on the floor, I'll give you the benefit of the doubt. Do you want to talk about it?"

I shake my head. "Not yet."

"Okay. Then what do you need from me? Distraction?"

This is why she's my best friend. She might show up uninvited, but she knows when not to push.

"Wanna just watch the movie with me? I need to see them get back together."

Lily gives me a smile of understanding. "You got it, babe."

When the end credits start to roll, Lily turns off the TV and turns to me. "We don't have to talk about you-know-who, but I do want to say one thing."

I gesture at her to go ahead. I knew she wouldn't be able to hold back completely.

"Serena filled me in on what happened last night. And I don't buy it, not for a second. Hunter is into you, so completely. Something spooked him. I'm not saying he wasn't a total dumbass, but that man is a goner for you."

"I know."

Lily's head rears back at my simple answer. "What do you know?"

"It's not my place to say. But I know he cares for me, just like I know there was more going on last night than I can tell you right now. He hurt me, big time, but I don't regret asking him to the gala, or going out on a date with him. Despite how I feel right now, I don't regret taking your dare and putting my heart on the line, even if he did break it a little bit." Lily squeezes my hand, and I brush away more tears. "Hunter Callaghan is a one in a million kind of guy. He's made me a better person, stronger, and he's shown me it's okay to be vulnerable."

"Oh, Kat," Lily whispers. But I keep going.

"Love hurts, Lily. It really freaking hurts sometimes. But you know what else hurts? Holding back feelings for someone out of fear. That's why I know I can forgive Hunter. Because I know how much he must be hurting right now. And if I can take away that pain, why wouldn't I do that for the man I love?"

Chapter Twenty

Hunter

Listen, I'm a big dude. I'm pretty strong, and as a cop, I know more than just the basics of de-escalation tactics and self-defense; I've done riot control before, and I've fired a gun.

None of that in any way prepared me for this.

Sitting in a conference room at the police station, staring across a table at three of the four Donnelly brothers and Leo. I wonder if this is what perps feel like when we interrogate them.

It fucking sucks.

The level of intensity in the glares being shot at me varies from curious to downright deadly.

But no matter how intimidated I am, I know I have to do this before I have any chance in hell of going after Kat. It's been three days since the night of the fundraiser, and it's been a constant battle not to run to her house and beg her to forgive me. But my daily sessions with Audrey have helped me realize I need to do this right. Which also means making it right with her family.

"Thanks for coming in today," I start, my voice wavering. I clear my throat and try again. If I'm going to show any vulnerability, it'll be by my own decision, not something stupid like my voice cracking. "I know I've got some explaining to do. But with respect, there's a lot of stuff I'm not gonna tell you because it's between me and your sister."

Max's eyebrows raise, Sawyer snorts, but Beckett and Leo just sit there. Cool, two out of four might not want to kill me outright.

"I have feelings for your sister. I have for a long fucking time, even back when she was with the dickwad who cheated on her. But I didn't act on it. Then, when she asked me to go to the gala with her, it gave me the courage to finally ask her out on a date. So no, I wasn't there as her friend. I was there as something more."

Wow. I got that out a lot calmer than I expected.

"Then why the fuck did you lie to our faces and break our sister's heart?" Sawyer barks out. Beckett, his twin, puts a hand on his arm but he shrugs it off. "This is exactly why we've always protected her. Because we *knew* some dumb fuck would come along and hurt her. We can't beat up Tyson since he lives too far away but we sure as shit can beat you up."

"Sawyer, shut up," Leo booms. "Last time I checked, we were all adults. No one is beating anyone up. You're not here to be a jackass to Hunter, you're here to listen to him. And if you can't do that, I will kick you out of my station."

Sawyer glowers at his cousin, but he does at least sink back in his chair. Leo faces me. "Go on, Callaghan."

This is it. This is when I have to come clean with them. It's a long shot no matter what, but if I don't, there isn't a chance in hell they'll understand.

"I have anxiety. Bad anxiety. And a learning disability," I start out quietly, my eyes glued to a spot on the table where someone let their coffee cup sit long enough it made a heat ring. "For most of my life, I've felt like I have to work extra hard to win people over because I'm not likable by myself. I have to be more. I believed I would never amount to anything and would never be worthy of loving someone."

Someone sighs. I think it's Beckett, but maybe it's Leo. He knew about my learning disability because he's my boss, but I guess I kept the anxiety pretty well under wraps.

"When I first met your sister, I knew I didn't have a chance of ever being good enough for her. But I couldn't stay away." I chance a look up at them, and the fact that even Sawyer is no longer looking like he wants to kill me is a shock. And gives me the motivation to continue. "She's amazing. You all know that better than me. Yeah, she didn't know about my anxiety, but she never treated me differently. She never made me feel stupid, or weak, or anything. Over time, she became so important to me, even if she had no clue. I hid my feelings for her, kept things friendly and neighbourly while she had a boyfriend, but she would smile, talk to me, laugh with me, and just make me feel normal. When I finally got up the courage to take things further..."

I trail off. Because this is where it gets tricky.

"When we took things further, I was the one who was terrified of telling you." I look Sawyer in the eyes. "I know how protective you are, and I knew I wouldn't measure up to your impossible standards. No one ever could. But even that wouldn't have stopped me from falling for her once she let me in her heart."

"So, you lied at the gala *because*?" Beckett asks quietly. I turn to him, relieved he's the one who asked the hardest question.

"Because I let my anxiety take over. Because I'm falling in love with Kat. No, fuck that, I *am* in love with Kat. She knows about my anxiety, and she didn't walk away from me; she stood beside me. And I'm ashamed to admit, I let her strength feed my insecurity instead of taming it."

"Well, that was dumb," Sawyer barks out. I wince at his choice of words, my gaze dropping down again. I don't see who smacks him, but I hear a muffled *thunk* and his muttered "ow."

"Yeah, it was," I say, forcing strength into my voice. Kat deserves nothing less from me. If I can't get through this without melting into an anxious puddle, what hope do I have of getting her to forgive me? I lift my head and fix my eyes on Sawyer. "It was dumb. But it happened and now I'm here, in front of all of you, trying to make it right. Because I want her back and proving to you that I deserve her is part of it. So how about you cut me a little bit of slack, Donnelly?"

"Finally," Leo mutters, and I cut my gaze to him, confused. His lips turn up slightly. "I've been waiting for you to realize that what we need to hear from you, see from you, is that you're man enough to stand up to these fuckers." He gestures to his cousins. "Because your anxiety is only a part of who you are. It doesn't make you weak. But not standing up for the woman you love would."

"I resent being lumped in with my idiotic twin," Beckett says mildly, "but Leo's right. I don't care that you have anxiety or a learning disability. I only care that you're man enough to stand up for Kat, for what makes her happy. And that's what you're doing now."

I blink slowly, unsure how this shift in the direction of our conversation happened. "How do you know I'm what makes her happy?" I ask hoarsely.

It's Max who answers, "We don't. Not really. But we're not blind, Hunter. We've all seen the way you two have danced around each other for a long time. And we all saw how devastated she was the night of the gala. It's not hard to put two and two together."

"Speak for yourself. I had no idea they liked each other," Sawyer grumbles, but he's softening, I think.

"Then you're the one who's being dumb. Even when she was with the dickwad, it was clear she liked Hunter," Max fires back. "So, I only have one question left."

I sit up straight. "I'll answer anything except questions about my relationship with Kat. That's between her and me."

Max's eyebrows raise, but in respect, not criticism. "Good response. But that wasn't what I was going to ask. I have zero desire to hear about my sister's love life. All I want to know is, what are you going to do to fix this with her?"

Turns out, Kat's brothers are good guys once you earn their trust and forgiveness. They had plenty of ideas on how to win her back, but in the end, I realized Kat doesn't need grand gestures. She needs honesty, transparency, and vulnerability.

Which is why I'm standing on her doorstep, feeling steadier than I have in days. She might not forgive me, but at least I know

I'm doing what's right.

When she opens the door, it takes everything I have not to pull her into my arms. God, she's beautiful, even with the dark circles under her eyes and her messy hair. Knowing I'm the cause of her hurting and not sleeping stabs me in the heart and strengthens my resolve to fix this.

"Hey, Kitty Kat," I say softly. "Can we talk?"

She nods, still not saying a word. Her silence is killing me, but I take the chance she gives me, following her into her house. When I see the mirror in her front hall, and I remember the things we did in front of it, my heart fills with love. Yeah, *love.* If things go well, I'm gonna tell her that.

Kat leans against the back of her couch, clutching her hands in front of her. Respecting her need for some space between us, I rest my shoulders against the wall opposite from her.

"I talked to your brothers this morning," I start, shoving my hands in my pockets. Facing them down was hard, but this is harder. "I apologized for lying and explained things to them. But not everything. Because they're not the ones who deserve to hear it, you are."

Audrey and I practiced this. Telling Kat about Becky, the bullies in school, nearly flunking out, and how all of that destroyed my self-esteem. How it all made me hide behind my armour of humour and charm.

"You're right, I do deserve that. I deserve the truth," she says, and I can hear the tremble in her voice. There's pain brimming underneath the surface, and I've never wanted to take away someone's hurt as badly as I do right now. But another thing Audrey said to me was that I had to give Kat the space to share her own feelings, not just share mine. Even if her feelings end up causing me more pain. So that's why, although it's killing me to stand here, silent, and not rush to apologize and beg for forgiveness, I don't.

"You hurt me, Hunter. Really, really hurt me. It took a lot of courage for me to put my heart out there again after Tyson cheated on me. And every time you held back, every time you hesitated on telling people about us, it felt as if you weren't as invested in our relationship as I was. But I kept ignoring my fears. I kept convincing myself you were in the same place as I was when it came to us. But what you did the other night? That destroyed me. It ruined my trust, not only in you, but in myself. Because how could I have been so wrong again?"

"You weren't wrong," I interrupt. "Babe, you weren't wrong. I am in this with you, fully, completely. I swear to God. Your heart isn't the only one on the line, mine is, too. I am so invested in us. That's part of why I freaked out so badly. Because losing you felt like the worst possible thing that could happen to me." I rake my hands through my hair. "I am so fucking sorry for hurting you, Kitty Kat. Please, can I try to explain what happened?"

She inclines her head toward me. Her posture is still stiff, defensive; I know I've got an uphill battle ahead of me. And it starts with honesty.

"In high school — before I knew the reason why I felt like I couldn't breathe before tests, like the walls were caving in, that I had an undiagnosed learning disability and out-of-control anxiety — there was a girl."

Kat's eyes flutter closed. When she opens them, the hurt that was there only a second ago is replaced with compassion. Her entire body softens, and I take it as a gesture for me to continue, so I do.

I tell her everything. About Becky, my anxiety, the medication I take, the therapy I'll probably always need. All of it. I tell her about how hard it is for me to go home, where Becky and everyone else who made me feel less than still reside.

And when I'm done, a weight I didn't even know I carried for all these years is lifted from my shoulders. I feel light, and I know, without a doubt, I'll always be a better man because of this moment. Because of her.

There's a heavy silence when I stop talking. Then Kat pushes off the couch and comes to stand in front of me. Slowly, hesitantly, her hand lifts and she rests it lightly on my chest. That simple touch sends heat searing through my body.

"I knew something must have happened to make it so hard for you to trust anyone. I'm sorry she made you think you weren't good enough. And I'm so sorry I didn't see your actions for what they were. I shouldn't have run from you." Her face is swimming with remorse and understanding. But the fact she feels guilty is not okay. Not after her earlier confession about how badly I broke her heart.

"No, Kitty Kat. You have nothing to be sorry for. I'm the one who screwed up and broke us." I lift my hand up to cup her cheek, but she shakes her head and steps back.

"You didn't break us, Hunter. And too bad because I am sorry." She folds her arms over her chest and stares at me, pain in her beautiful eyes. Pain for me, not because of me. "I shouldn't have pushed so hard for us to tell everyone before you were ready. If I'd given you more time, if we had longer to build our own connection and trust, maybe none of this would have happened."

I sigh, the sound laced with regret. "It wouldn't have mattered how long we waited. I was so fucked up when it came to how I thought I measured up against you; I don't know if I would have ever been ready. I'm the only one who should be apologizing for ever making you doubt my feelings. Because they're real, Kitty Kat. So fucking real, it's terrifying and amazing all at the same time. I promise you, I will never make you question that, ever again."

Her eyes soften and thank fuck, she finally steps back toward me and wraps her arms around my waist. I don't waste the opportunity, yanking her into my embrace and crushing her to me.

"Hunter, there's no measuring needed. I see your demons and they don't frighten me. I want the best of you and the worst of you. You just need to let me in, so I can fight those shadows with you." She tilts her head up to look at me, and what I see written in her eyes has my heart bursting, in a good way.

"I know. I get that now. I'm just so fucking sorry it took me screwing up and hurting you to figure that out. Is there any way you can forgive me? Can we move forward?" I ask, hopeful, yet terrified at the same time. This is it. "I really am so sorry, Kat."

"I know you are. And I won't let us be defined by our past mistakes if you won't."

I let out a shaky exhale and open my mouth to speak but she covers it with her hand.

"No more apologies, okay? We're only going to get stuck in a Canadian standoff, and I can think of much better ways to show our forgiveness instead of getting caught in a loop of 'I'm sorry's.'"

There's a twinkle in her eyes that both soothes me and turns me on. And when she smiles that little smirk that promises all kinds of dirty things? I'm a goner.

Goddamn, this woman. I'm so in love with her.

Chapter Twenty-One

Kat

I'm not trying to trivialize Hunter's confession or our apologies to each other when I make my suggestion to him. I just want to cement our connection the best way I know how, and that's with our bodies. There's no doubt, no questioning, no room for worries or anxiety when we come together. And I know he sees that when he grabs me around my waist and lifts me up into his arms. My legs wrap around his body and finally our lips meet in a kiss that erases any lingering guilt or pain.

"Kat, I need to tell you this," Hunter starts to say in between kisses. I chase after his mouth with my own, not needing to hear anymore words to know how I feel. "Babe. Please."

I lean back in his arms, loving his strength and the ease with which he holds me. "You better walk and talk, buddy. Because I want to be naked in bed with you in less than ten seconds."

His mouth flaps open and shut a couple of times before a slow, sexy smile creeps across his face. But Hunter doesn't move.

"Hunter. Bedroom, now." I say, trying to inject some sort of authority into my voice. My hand slaps ineffectively against his muscled shoulder. I might as well be trying to move a brick wall.

"It's cute you think you're in charge right now, Kitty Kat," he says, his tone way too fucking casual. I narrow my eyes at him and start to squirm, hoping he'll put me down. But I should know better.

"I said, I need to tell you something. And I need to tell you this *before* I strip your clothes off your body and make you come with my fingers, my tongue, and my cock."

My body shudders in his arms and the heat that was starting to coil inside of me grows into an inferno.

Hunter tilts his head to the side and smirks at me. "Do I have your attention now?"

I nod, my tongue darting out to moisten my lips.

"Good. Because this is important." He shifts slightly, somehow managing to hold me up with one arm so his free hand can come up to cup my cheek. "I love you, Kat Donnelly. And I need you to hear that now, not later, so you know this isn't my dick talking, it's my heart. Or maybe I should say *your* heart because you own mine."

Well, shoot. Now I'm crying.

His thumb comes up to gently swipe away the tear that falls down my cheek. "Happy tears?" The smallest thread of uncertainty is in those two words. It's now my mission to erase them completely.

I nod emphatically. "I love you, too. And you've got my heart, too."

Finally, we're moving, and seconds later, Hunter drops me on my bed, following right after so his body hovers over me.

"Say it again."

I lift my hands to cup his jaw and stare deep into his eyes that seem to be shining with unshed tears, just like mine. "I love you, Hunter. All of you."

"I love you." His lips crash into mine, his body pinning me to the bed. "God, I love you."

I push against his chest, and we make our way to sitting. Clothes start to fly everywhere as our movements turn frantic, as if the world might end if we don't get naked immediately.

And when he's bared to me, I finally manage to turn the tables on Hunter and flip him onto his back, swinging my legs up and over so I'm straddling him. My hands come to his chest, and I hold him down, locking my gaze on his. I can feel his erection between my legs, getting coated in my own arousal, but this is more important.

"When I say I love all of you, I mean everything. The good stuff and the hard stuff. Do you trust me on that? Do you believe me when I say I'll still love you when things seem dark?"

That tear I saw filling his eyes earlier spills over and he lifts a hand to brush it away. "Yeah," he says, his voice hoarse with emotion. "I trust you. I believe you."

"Good. You make me feel like anything is possible. And I promise, I will always do my best to make you feel that way, too. Because if we're together, then it's the truth."

I bend down, and starting at his forehead, I begin to pepper kisses over his face, erasing his tears with my love. And I don't stop there. I kiss my way down his body until I reach his cock. I grasp it in my hand and look up at his chocolate eyes. That uncertainty from before is gone and pure lust — and love — is there instead.

Mission accomplished.

"I love you, Hunter Callaghan."

I wrap my lips around the tip of his cock, and slowly, I begin to move my head, up and down, swirling my tongue over the tip before starting again. Over and over, until his hands are gripping my hair tightly and his body is taut with tension underneath me.

"Babe. I need to come," he growls, lifting me off his cock and yanking me up the length of his body.

I lift a finger up to wipe my mouth, keeping my eyes glued to his face. Fire burns in his eyes and it's all for me. I lean over, letting my breasts graze his chest as I reach for the unopened box of condoms Lily left as a parting gift the night of the gala. Taking one out, I open it and roll it down his rigid length. Then finally, I lift my hips, grasp him in my hands again, and line his cock up with my entrance.

With his hands on my hips, guiding me, I rock up and down, taking more of him each time, until finally I'm filled with him. I lower my head and kiss him, and the second our lips meet, he takes over. His grip on me tightens and his hips begin to thrust up, pushing us impossibly closer.

"God, yes," I moan, my hands grasping the pillow on either side of his head.

"Wrong name," Hunter grunts, wrapping my hair around one hand as he levers us both up into a sitting position. God, I love feeling him like this. The angle drives him in even deeper, and I cry out as my orgasm hits me like a lightning bolt.

"Fuck, Kat. Babe. You're everything. You're fucking everything." Hunter roars out my name as his own release takes over and he pistons up into me over and over again.

My arms are wrapped tightly around him, and his are around

me, and we sit there, entwined in each other for several minutes as our heartbeats return to normal.

Eventually, he slowly shifts me to the side, his cock slipping out of me. He kisses my forehead, then climbs out of bed and heads to the bathroom, returning shortly after and crawling into my bed. I settle back into his arms, and he pulls the blanket up from the bottom of the bed to cover us.

I've never felt as safe, and loved, and cherished as I do right now in Hunter's arms. I come from an affectionate family and there was no shortage of hugs growing up. But this right here, the intimacy of our naked bodies tangled up in each other, sticky with sweat and passion, this is the deepest connection I've ever felt with another person in my entire life.

I know Hunter and I have work to do to make sure this connection stays strong. But I also know we can do it — together. Which means, as his partner, I'm hoping he'll let me in just a little bit more. I lift onto my elbow and look down at his handsome face.

"Would it be okay for me to join one of your therapy sessions some day? I'd really like to talk to Audrey and make sure I know the very best way to support you."

Hunter's brows raise in surprise as he lifts onto his elbow as well, his hand finding mine in between our bodies. "You'd do that? Really?"

"Of course, I would. I mean, I know you can also tell me what I can do, but I just thought maybe it would be easier for you if she told me. But only whatever you're comfortable with."

He pulls me so I'm spread out on top of him, happiness seeping out of him. "Babe, I'm an open book for you. No more secrets. You can know anything. But yeah —" a shy smile crosses his face "— I'd really like it if you met with me and Audrey. Because I want this to work between us. And that means I'm gonna need her help to keep my anxiety under control. So I can be strong for you."

I stroke back the piece of hair I've longingly wanted to touch for so long. "Hunter, you *are* strong. So strong. No matter what, don't doubt that. But we can be stronger, together."

He kisses me deeply. But before we can get lost in each other again, I push against his chest, lifting myself slightly. "And you're staying here tonight. All night. Got it?"

The light in his eyes grows, as does his smile. "Got it. All night."

I don't want to open my eyes in case this is a dream.

That's my first thought waking up this morning. The second is the realization that the wall of heat I feel at my back is coming from a man. The same man whose arms are tightly banded around me, whose legs are tangled with mine, and whose lips I feel against my hair.

"Morning, Kitty Kat."

A smile works its way across my face. *It's not a dream.* I twist and roll over to face him.

"You're here."

He gives me a sleepy smile. "Yup." His arms tighten, and he crushes me to his body. "I promised all night. And I'm never going to break a promise to you again."

My alarm goes off, interrupting what's already shaping up to be the most perfect morning ever. I stretch over Hunter to turn it off. "I have to volunteer at the shelter today." His hand comes up and pushes my hair away from my face, and I tilt my cheek into his touch. "Will you come with me?"

His grin grows broader. "You couldn't keep me away today if you tried. I just got you back, there's not a chance in hell I'm letting you out of my sight for a while."

It's so over-the-top, I giggle. "What about work?"

Somehow, he manages to lift one brow. "I have handcuffs."

"Oh my God." I laugh harder now, pushing against him to try and get up. "You're not handcuffing us together."

He follows me out of bed, his hands coming back around my waist as he drops a kiss to my shoulder "I'm also not losing you again."

I turn around and cup his face in my hands. "No, you're not. Because I love you."

Our kiss is sweet and soft, but full of everything those three words mean to us. I know we've got work to do for both of us to overcome the things that held us back, that trapped us in fear and doubt. But I also know with complete certainty that we can do it together.

"Now c'mon, I don't want to be late."

An hour later, we're on the floor of the Dogwood Cove Animal Shelter with three curious kittens climbing all over our laps. And let me be the first one to say, a big burly police officer holding a tiny purring kitten up to his cheek is just about the cutest thing ever.

"You need a pet," I say as Hunter puts down one kitten, only to pick up another.

"I would love a dog, but with shift work, I wouldn't be able to care for it properly. What about you?"

I look down at the little grey cat who's curled up asleep in my lap. She climbed up there when we first arrived and hasn't left. "I've always wanted a cat or dog. We had pets growing up, but my ex was allergic to pet dander."

"What's stopping you now?"

I consider his question, coming up empty. "I honestly don't know."

Hunter's eyes glint. "I mean, do I need to say those three words?"

I glare at him. "Don't even think about daring me, Hunter Callaghan." He throws his head back and laughs, and the sound of his happiness fills the room.

"Okay, I won't. But you should think about it." He gestures to the kitten purring in my lap. "Princess Sparkles needs a home."

I arch a brow at him. "Excuse me? Princess what?"

"It's a good name."

"It's terrible."

Hunter gives a mock gasp. "I'm hurt, Kitty Kat. You're insulting my name choice?"

We both dissolve into laughter for several more minutes before I realize my shift is over and it's time to go. I lift the grey kitten up to my face and press a kiss to her perfect pink nose.

"Someday, I'll take one of these babies home."

CHAPTER TWENTY-TWO

Hunter

Christmas Eve has always been my favourite day of the year. As a kid, it was for obvious reasons. The anticipation for Christmas morning was the best part. But as an adult, my reason for loving December twenty-fourth has changed.

With my family doing all their celebrating on the twenty-fifth, the day before became the day I shut myself off from the world. Totally disconnected — no phone, no internet, nothing. I would give myself twenty-four hours to let go of any stress or worry and be completely selfish. I'd sit around in my underwear, pig out on my favourite food, and play video games or watch TV. I wouldn't think about my job, my family, or anything.

This year, I'm loving Christmas Eve for a totally different reason, and she's lying in bed next to me, her hair tickling my chest. It's been seven days since I went to Kat's house to ask for her forgiveness. Seven days since I bared my soul to her, showed her every insecurity, every fear, every weakness. And it's been seven days since she looked me in the eyes and told me she loved me, no matter what.

It's also been seven nights of us falling asleep together, and seven mornings of us waking up together. And those mornings have been the best mornings of my life.

"Mmm." Her arms tighten around me as Kat nuzzles her face into my pec. "Why are you awake so early?" she mumbles.

"Because it's the best day of the year, Kitty Kat," I whisper, my lips pressed against the top of her head. "And this year is the best year ever, so it's extra best."

She lifts her head and squints at me. "Extra best?"

I nod solemnly, fighting back my grin. "Yup. Extra best. Because this year, you get to experience the wonder of Christmas Eve, Hunter style." Although, I did break with tradition in one small way, and we will be having a quick visit from someone later this morning. Kat doesn't know about that, though.

She rolls away from my body and stretches, her back arching off the bed, pushing her perfect tits up in the air. Being the red-blooded male I am, and being obsessed with her body, it's impossible not to bend down and cover one with my mouth.

"Hunter," Kat moans, her hands tangling in my hair, holding me in place.

As if I would want to move. Crazy girl.

I cover her body with mine and rub up and down, making sure she feels every inch of delicious friction. Given the way she shivers and shudders underneath me, mission accomplished.

I make my way down, kissing every inch of skin my lips can reach, until I finally settle between her legs. "Mmm. Merry Christmas to me," I say, waggling my eyebrows up at her. Kat giggles, covering her eyes with her hand until I reach up and pull it away. "Uh-uh, babe. You know the rule."

Her eyes darken with lust. Turns out, my girl is a bit of a

voyeur and the fastest way to get her arousal ramped up to 100 percent is having her watch. Whether it's me going down on her, or my dick sliding in and out of her pussy, Kat gets off on the visual.

And I am more than happy to encourage that.

After making sure her eyes are locked on me, I kiss the inside of each of her thighs before lifting them up and draping them over my shoulders, opening her to me.

"I will never get tired of this," I mumble, leaning in and pressing the lightest of kisses to her pubic bone. She twitches, her hips shifting, trying to get me where she wants me. "This perfect, perfect pussy." With each word, I stroke up and down with my finger, coming closer to where she wants me. "And it's mine, isn't it, Kitty Kat? It's all mine."

"Yes, Hunter. It's yours. Now please, *please* make me come!"

Her voice rises into a plaintive cry as I suck her clit into my mouth. Out of the corner of my eye, I can see she's watching, her big brown eyes locked on what I'm doing. I reach up and grab her hand, bringing it to the back of my head. Because goddamn, do I love it when she loses control and fucks my face.

Moments later, we both get what we want as Kat grinds her pussy into my mouth, screaming out my name as I lick up every fucking drop of her orgasm.

"You really do know how to wake a girl up, don't you," Kat teases as I pull myself up to lie on the bed beside her. My hand draws lazy circles on her stomach, and I'm sure what is a very satisfied smirk covers my face.

"Only the right girl."

She rolls onto her side. "Good answer."

Leaning in, I let Kat kiss me. But when she reaches down and wraps her hand around my dick, I pull back.

"Can't believe I'm gonna say this, but we don't have time for that."

She lifts her eyebrows and runs her hand up and down my length once more. "Really? Not even a quickie?"

I sigh dramatically. "No. Unfortunately not." I roll over to the edge of the bed and sit up, looking back at her with an over-the-top woeful expression. "Trust me, right now, I'm regretting the plans I put in place." I glance down at my cock jutting straight out in front of me. "Really regretting them."

Kat climbs out of bed and struts around to my side of the bed, standing between my legs in all her perfect naked glory. "These plans better be amazing if you're giving up sex for them. But I thought today was all about disconnecting from the outside world? What plans did you make?"

My hands lift up to cup her perfect tits that just happen to be at eye level. "It's really hard to remember when I'm staring at what I love most in the world."

"You love my boobs the most in the world?"

I nod sagely. "Yup." I look up at her with a grin. "They're very important to me."

She steps back and my hands fall.

"What about the rest of me?" she asks saucily. I tilt my head to the side, pretending to consider her question.

"I mean, I guess I love all of you, but those tits." I lick my lips. "Mmm."

Kat rolls her eyes, but I see her smile. "You're ridiculous."

"But you love me." Shit, does it feel good to say that with total confidence. Because I don't doubt for a second that Kat loves me.

"I do." She steps forward again, leans down, and presses a far too brief kiss to my upturned lips. "Do these plans of yours at least allow for me to have a shower and some coffee?"

I rise off the bed, grabbing Kat by the waist and tossing her over my shoulder, grinning at her shriek of laughter when I turn my head and bite her ass gently as I walk to her bathroom. "We better shower together to save time."

Showering together didn't save time. In fact, we've only just managed to get dressed, and I'm chasing a giggling Kat down the hall to the kitchen when there's a knock at her door.

"I got the door," I call out, pivoting to head to the door. "You start the coffee."

I open the front door to a grinning Mila and her husband Jackson, who's hovering behind her. She's holding a box in front of her.

"Hey guys," I say, stepping out into the cold and pulling the door mostly shut behind me. "You got the goods?"

"Yup. Has she guessed anything?"

I shake my head, my smile covering my face. Jackson steps forward and puts a large bag on the porch. "Everything you'll need for the first week is in there."

"Awesome. Thanks for dropping it off." I take the box from Mila, resisting the urge to peek inside. "Merry Christmas."

Mila and Jackson each give me a wave, then turn to make their way back to Jackson's truck. I bend down, balancing the box in one arm, and grabbing the bag in the other before nudging the front door open. Setting the bag down just inside, I close the door, lock it, and make my way to the kitchen.

"Who was it?" Kat asks, her back to me as she does something by the kitchen sink. I quickly put the box down on the kitchen table, open it, and lift out what's inside just as she turns to face me. Her eyes go immediately to the bundle of dark grey fur in my arms.

"Hunter," she says breathlessly, "Why are you holding a kitten?"

"Merry Christmas, Kitty Kat."

"What?" the love of my life asks, finally lifting her gaze to meet mine. Unshed tears are shining in her eyes. "Is this…"

I simply nod before placing the adorable fuzzball in Kat's open hands. When we went together the other day to volunteer at the animal shelter for a few hours, Kat fell in love with the abandoned kitten that was waiting for a new home. I knew right then, I had to do this. Thankfully, Mila was a willing accomplice. Just like everyone else in town, she accepted Kat and I being together without question.

"Yep. I couldn't leave Princess Sparkles all alone in the shelter over Christmas, now, could I? Besides. You're the perfect cat-mom for this little girl. She might've had a rough start to life, but I know better than anyone that Kat Donnelly can make anyone stronger and better than ever."

Kat's eyes are dancing as she lightly slaps my arm. "That is *not* her name. Her name is Gigi."

My shoulders lift in a shrug as my lips quirk up. "Fine, Gigi."

I couldn't care less about the kitten's name, not when Kat looks so damn happy.

"Hunter," Kat murmurs as she nuzzles the kitten. "I love her. Thank you." She reaches one arm out to cup my head behind my neck, pulling me in close. "And I love you." Our lips meet in a sweet kiss, one that I don't want to end, but there's more I need to say.

"Kat, I was lovestruck the second I laid eyes on you. This might sound crazy and like I'm moving way too fast. But I don't care. I want forever with you, and someday soon, it won't be a kitten I'm giving you as a gift, it'll be a diamond ring."

Careful not to crush the tiny kitten purring between our bodies, I kiss her again. When tiny claws dig into my skin, we part. Kat readjusts Gigi, lifting her up to press a kiss to her tiny pink nose before setting her down on the ground. With both of her arms free, she wraps them around my waist and pulls me in close before staring up at me with love shining from her eyes.

"Forever sounds good to me."

Epilogue

Kat

"I swear to God, if he isn't back soon, I might explode."

My mom makes a sound of understanding from the other end of the phone line. "Patience, sweetie. Everything is going to be fine."

Easy for her to say. She's not the one who had to deal with her boyfriend dry heaving with anxiety this morning. I continue pacing the living room, my phone pressed to my ear, as I anxiously wait for Hunter to get home.

"He was so worried this morning, for no reason. It's hard, Mom, sometimes I just don't know how to get through to him and make him realize he has nothing to worry about."

"You can't always fix things, Kat, sometimes you're just going to have to love him through the hard stuff. Just like we're all doing with Max right now."

I hear the worry in her voice when she mentions my older brother, and my own heart squeezes. Something's got the oldest Donnelly tied up in knots, and we all can see it. It's been a couple of weeks now, and at family dinners he's distant, like his mind is lost in thought. When he does talk, he's short and grumpy.

Which is not normal for him. I asked the twins about it; Sawyer claimed to know nothing, except that it started the day the new round of residents began their rotation at the hospital. That doesn't surprise me, he's the worst at keeping secrets, so none of us tell him anything we want kept quiet. But I'm positive Beckett or Jude must know more, since that's who Max would confide in out of all of us, but they aren't saying anything.

"He'll come to us when he's ready." I inject some optimism into my words.

"He will. Your father and I worked hard to raise the five of you to be strong, independent adults who know when to ask for help. Hopefully, Max will do just that when he needs to. Now you, my darling girl, need to hang up the phone and get ready to congratulate Hunter when he walks in the door."

I hang up, take a deep breath, and think about what she said. She's right, of course, and I do know that already. I know the best thing I can do for Hunter is stand by his side through whatever he experiences. But days like today, when he's *this* close to reaching a dream he wouldn't let himself admit to having, I want to erase all his fears and make him see he deserves this.

He deserves everything.

Just then, the door opens and Hunter bursts through, a wide grin on his face.

"You're looking at Detective Callaghan of the Dogwood Cove Police Department." He swings me off my feet and around in a circle.

Getting here took a lot of hard work. It began right after Christmas, when we had a video call with his parents, and his mom had mentioned the detective position. Hunter's avoidance of her question surprised me. So, after the call, I told him what Leo had said to me weeks before at the café. And just as he promised he would, Hunter let me in, and shared his anxieties with me. Together, and with Audrey's help, we worked through his insecurities and false beliefs about himself. And then last week, he did it. He went to Leo and asked to be considered, even though it was well past the deadline.

Which brought us to today, when he had to sit down with the chief, Leo, and the deputy commissioner from Westport, for his interview. I couldn't tell him that Leo had all but assured me Hunter was guaranteed the position. Leo made me promise not to, saying it wouldn't be professional. But my cousin also knew how Hunter would be struggling, and he'd need me to be strong. Although it was hard not to reassure him this morning, I knew Hunter had to go through with things this way, to face his demons.

"Thank you, Kitty Kat," he says when we finally separate. "You did this. You got me here."

I stroke back the piece of hair that is mine to touch whenever I want. "No, you did the hard work. I just gave you the nudge to step out of fear and into possibility."

"You loved me. That was all the nudge I needed."

His simple statement has tears brimming in my eyes. "I do love you. And I'm so proud of you."

He sets me down, and cradles my face in his hands, holding me as if I'm his most precious possession. Which is how he always makes me feel — loved, cherished, adored.

"You know what?" he whispers, and to my surprise, I see tears building in his eyes. "I'm proud of myself."

I let out a small gasp. "Oh Hunter," I murmur.

He kisses me firmly once, twice, then pulls away, bringing his hands down to clasp mine. "I wouldn't be here without you, Kat. You said once that we were stronger together, and you were right. I never in a million years saw myself with someone who accepts me, all of me. But you do. You have a gift for making people see the very best in themselves. And I promise, I will spend the rest of my life dedicated to showing you how amazing that is, how amazing you are."

When he kisses me again, I feel the conviction behind his words. He believes in me, and in himself.

He believes in us.

"This promotion means you're stuck with me." His voice takes on a teasing quality.

"That's just fine with me. But that means you're stuck with my family."

His hands drop mine as if they're on fire. "Uh-oh. Hold on, I need to rethink this." He steps back, mock horror on his face.

The twinkle in his eyes gives away his true feelings, as if I would ever doubt him. Still, I play along, placing one hand on my hip and tilting my head at him. "Yep, a lifetime of family dinners with my brothers. Can't you see it now?"

Hunter swoops back in, picking me up and tossing me over his shoulder. I swat at his back, laughing as he carries me down the hallway to my bedroom. Once we're there, he slides me down his body before threading his fingers through my hair and tipping my face up to meet his. "I can handle a lifetime of anything, as long as I have you."

"Good. 'Cause you've got me."

"That's all I needed to hear. I love you, Kitty Kat."

Are you desperate for more Donnellys? Kat and Hunter have an exclusive bonus scene that you can get here: **https://bit.ly/Ju liaJarrett_DTKY_bonus**

Acknowledgments

Writing this version of Kat and Hunter's story was not something I anticipated doing. Until, that is, I finished their novella and immediately wished I could have written more. The holiday version, Lovestruck, resonated with many readers, especially Hunter's struggles. And when comments started coming in, telling me how they wanted more as well, I knew I had to do it.

Special thanks for this version goes to Theresa Leigh, who gave me her expert guidance and advice on how best to expand their story and have it make sense in the bigger **Donnellys of Dogwood Cove** series.

As always, my author friends, my family, and my team kept me in line, on time, and moderately sane. Chelle, Amy, Molly, Claire, Georgia, Mae, Theresa, Alex, Chris and Carolina, thank you for being by my side!

And you, dear reader. I hope you find light and hope in this story. If it reflects something that you yourself have experienced, know that you are not alone. Believe that even the darkest of moments can turn light again.

With all my love, Julia.

ALSO BY JULIA JARRETT

<u>Dogwood Cove</u>

Always and Forever

Rumours and Romance

Work and Play

Truth and Temptation

Then and Now

Passion and Promises: A Dogwood Cove Novella Collection

<u>The Donnellys of Dogwood Cove</u>

Dare To Kiss You

Hate To Want You

Pretend To Love You

Promise To Marry You

Dare To Marry You: A Donnellys of Dogwood Cove Holiday

Novella

One Night To Win You

<u>Standalone</u>

Seductive Swimmer - A standalone novel set in the Cocky Hero

World, inspired by Vi Keeland and Penelope Ward's Cocky Bas-

tard series

About Julia Jarrett

Julia Jarrett is a busy mother of two boys, a happy wife to her real-life book boyfriend and the owner of two rescue dogs, one from Guatemala and another one from Taiwan. She lives on the West Coast of Canada and when she isn't writing contemporary romance novels full of relatable heroines and swoon-worthy heroes, she's probably drinking tea (or wine) and reading.

For a complete listing of Julia Jarrett books please visit
www.authorjuliajarrett.com/books

<u>Follow Julia:</u>
Instagram @juliajarrettauthor
Facebook Reader Group: Julia Jarrett's Nutty Muffins
TikTok @julia.jarrett.author